How To
Ensnare a
Highlander

The MacGregor Lairds

How To Ensnare a Highlander

The MacGregor Lairds

Michelle McLean

Entangled Publishing, LLC
2614 South Timberline Road
Suite 105, PMB 159
Fort Collins, CO 80525
Visit our website at www.entangledpublishing.com.

Scandalous is an imprint of Entangled Publishing, LLC.

Edited by Erin Molta
Cover design by Erin Dameron-Hill
Cover art from Period Images and Deposit Photos

Manufactured in the United States of America

First Edition February 2018

SCANDALOUS

To Silver Blade,
the first floppy-haired highwayman to steal my young,
hopelessly romantic heart

Chapter One

Lady Elizabet Harding gripped the reins of her horse tighter, blood thundering in her ears as the nervous animal twitched beneath her.

"It's all right, girl. It's only a bit of thunder. It will pass. We'll be home soon enough...as long as we keep moving." She tried to keep her voice calm and soothing. A difficult task, with several hundred pounds of horse, tense and ready to bolt beneath her.

She had no one to blame but herself, of course, for insisting on riding out with a storm looming—without a groom. She'd desperately needed the escape, though. While she normally enjoyed visiting friends in the country, especially so far north where they were completely away from all the bustle of the court in London, it also meant more frequent attention from her parents. If she had to listen to her mother drone on about her duty to her family one more time, or hear Lord Dawsey go on about how the family was on the brink of ruin, thanks to that dreadful Highland Highwayman who was terrorizing the roads, she'd go mad.

Elizabet had heard the stories. That the Highland Highwayman was a regular Robin Hood, stealing from the rich and returning his gains to the poor. If it were true, she stood firmly on the highwayman's side. Frankly, the fact that the highwayman and his band of rogues had intercepted no less than three of the wagons carrying the rents from her father's estates didn't make half the dent in their fortunes as Lord Dawsey's own vices. Besides, she'd seen her father's tenants. They could use all the coin they could get.

Still, she could understand the strain it put on her father. Though that didn't mean she wanted to be sold off to the highest bidder in order to replenish her family's fortunes. Her mother, either oblivious of Elizabet's distress or simply uncaring, refused to quit harping on the matter. And so Elizabet now sat on a terrified horse, pelted by rain, and in danger of being struck by lightning or thrown from the poor animal when it bolted.

"Easy, girl," she said, patting the mare's neck.

Unfortunately, a peal of thunder rolled through, burying her words in a cacophony of booming rumbles.

The mare jumped, shooting forward so rapidly it yanked the slippery, wet reins from Elizabet's hands. She buried them instead in the horse's mane and held on for dear life. The terrified animal was beyond hearing her now.

The horse bolted straight for the shelter of the trees, which might not have been a horrible idea except for the branches that lashed at Elizabet's body. A particularly tenacious branch whipped out and snagged her hair, ripping it from its pins. She buried her face in her arms the best she could and debated the merits of jumping. Surely, doing so would cause less damage than being pummeled to death by the prickly trees.

"Ho there!"

The voice echoed faintly through the woods, growing stronger as it repeated.

The steady pounding of hooves against the ground joined the sound of her own horse, and Elizabet risked a glance up.

"Hold tight!"

Through the wet and tangled curtain of her hair, she could see only the blur of a man astride a great black stallion as he pulled alongside her and reached for the reins. The trees kept getting in the way, thwarting his attempts and causing him to veer off. Finally, he brought his horse as close to hers as possible and reached over again. His arms wrapped around her waist and he deftly pulled her to his horse, settling her across his kilted lap.

She uttered a startled squeak and held onto him for dear life.

"Whoa, whoa there," he said, reining in his own horse.

"Thank you," Elizabet said. She vaguely wondered if there was some formal etiquette involved in thanking a strange man for saving one's life from a runaway horse, but promptly decided she didn't care.

"My pleasure, lass," he said.

A Scot for sure, though the kilted plaid he wore instead of breeches had betrayed that fact before he'd uttered a word. "You're a long way from home," she said, intrigued at the mysterious man who still held her close.

She shoved her hair out of her face, happy to be safe and sound and in the arms of…

She shrieked and tried to scramble away, but there was nowhere to go. The man held her tightly, probably a good thing, else she'd have toppled from the horse. Though that might have been better than remaining in the grasp of a highwayman.

"Easy, lass. I'll no' hurt ye," he said, talking to her like he would a skittish colt.

He might have done better to address the horse. Her caterwauling and thrashing about spooked the animal, and they were off again.

"Hold still, ye daft wee loon! Ye'll see both our necks broken!"

"Then let me go!" she yelled, trying to shove him away, though he was somehow managing to maintain his hold on her while keeping them both astride. The horse, however, didn't care for the skirmish taking place on his back and reared up. Elizbet found herself crushed between the highwayman and the horse's neck as the former tightened his grip to keep them both from falling.

She stopped struggling. More because she didn't wish to break a bone falling from the massive horse than because she trusted the masked man who held her. The brief reprieve allowed the highwayman to settle the horse long enough for them to slide off its back.

She darted away but he lunged, blocking her escape. She moved back, keeping the horse between them.

"What do you want?" she asked, reaching out to touch the stallion. The last thing she wanted was to be gut-kicked by a startled animal.

The man gazed at her with a pair of eyes the color of robin's eggs. Eyes that seemed kind and crinkled at the corners with a smile when he spoke. Eyes she'd trust…if they weren't shadowed by a mask.

"I wanted only to keep ye from breaking that lovely neck of yours. And that's a fine way to thank a man for saving yer life. Screeching so to wake the dead, and right in my ear. 'Tis a wonder I'm not deaf."

She slowly made her way to the left, but he tracked her every movement. "Fine. Thank you. You may go now."

He shook his head with a growing grin. "Nay, lass. I'll no'

go and leave ye alone in the forest with a storm raging. No matter what ye may think of my company. Now. Will ye get back on the horse or do ye want me to throw ye across it like a sack of flour? Ye canna stay out here or ye'll catch yer death."

She glared at him, but with the rain continuing to pelt down and bolts of lightning still striking at terrifyingly regular intervals, she had little choice but to stop fighting. Her lack of say in the matter made her bite her lip in frustration.

"Very well. I'll ride," she said, through gritted teeth.

He bowed and then grasped her around the waist, hoisting her onto the stallion's back before she had half a second to rethink her answer. He mounted behind her and wrapped his arms around her once again. She held her body stiff for the first while, but maintaining that position while swaying on a horse proved more difficult than she anticipated. After a few more minutes, she gave in and slumped against him.

"Bit of an odd day for a ride, aye?"

The comment startled a laugh out of her. "Yes, well, the weather was fine when I set out. And I didn't expect to venture quite this far."

"Aye, well horses do tend to have a mind of their own on occasion."

Elizabet frowned, worry for her mare rippling through her. "Will she be all right?"

"Och, aye. They ken where to go when the weather is foul. More than I can say for a few runaway lassies."

She glared at him and he laughed, the deep sound reverberating through his chest and into her own. She found herself leaning into it, wanting to soak up the mirth emanating from this man. Her own life sported a sad lack of happy people. Then she remembered the good-humored man holding her was a masked outlaw, and she returned to her rigid position.

He steered his horse through the trees until they reached

a rock outcrop with an overhanging ledge large enough for them to fit beneath.

"Well. It's no' much as far as shelter goes. But it'll keep the rain off ye, at least."

She said nothing, though she was grateful for the shelter. Thanking a criminal seemed the wrong thing to do. Even if he *had* saved her sorry skin and had been nothing but a gentleman. So far.

She still shivered from the cold, but at least the rocks blocked the worst of the wind and offered the vast improvement of keeping the rain from blowing in her face.

He dismounted, reached his arms up for her, and she allowed him to help her down. He held her slightly longer than strictly necessary and stared at her, searching her face.

"Ye've a few scratches on yer cheek," he said, pulling a soft handkerchief from his vest and lightly brushing it across her skin.

She jerked away but he persisted. "They must be cleansed unless ye wish for them to become inflamed. Maybe scar. 'Twould be a shame to mar such beauty."

The compliment sent a warm flutter through her belly. The threat of a scar held her steady, though his ministrations stung a bit. He must be the Highland Highwayman. Gallant, charming, and handsome, as far as could be told with his face and hair mostly covered by a hat, kerchief, and mask. But a thief, nonetheless. A lawless criminal who would probably relieve her of any valuables she possessed as payment for saving her life.

Still, she couldn't help the sheer exhilaration streaking through her. To meet the notorious highwayman in person. The tales of his charm were certainly true. Her heart thundered beneath her rib cage as he dabbed at her cheek. No other man in her life would have treated her with such gentleness and care, tenderly wiping at her cuts and scrapes.

No other person at all, really. Despite her suspicion of his intentions—the man *was* an outlaw, after all—a sense of gratitude, and longing, filled her.

"Thank you," she said, taking the handkerchief from him and holding it to her cheek. She belatedly realized she still stood in the circle of his arms and moved back a few steps. His lips twitched in amusement.

"I'll see what can be done about a fire."

She nodded and took the horse's reins, leading him farther under the rock ledge. With her back to the rock and the horse in front of her, she was protected from the worst of the wind. She wrapped her cloak tighter about her and watched the man search the area for the driest wood he could find.

He worked for several minutes with the flint and steel and bit of char cloth he'd dug from his sporran and before too long had a small fire going with a stack of slightly damp wood he'd found in the underbrush. He motioned her over.

"Come warm yerself."

She went eagerly, though she kept a safe distance between them when she sat, holding her chilled hands out to the subtle heat thrown off by the flames.

"You are handy to have in an emergency, aren't you?" she said.

He gave her a crooked grin and a little bow in return. "I do what I can, my lady."

She watched him move about the fire, gathering twigs to make it larger, and tried to think of a solution to her current situation. Lost in the forest with a mysterious and dangerous man. Though never, in all the stories she'd heard of the Highland Highwayman, had there been talk of him mistreating a woman. Oh, he'd stolen with alacrity and left his victims poorer. But not harmed. And many of the women who he'd come in contact with had been quite taken with him.

Elizabet could see why. He'd become something of a romantic legend, even though face-to-face the real man did inspire more fear than she'd imagined. Though, she was honest enough to admit to herself, that the danger surrounding him was part of the appeal.

But as he had been nothing but chivalrous with her, and had, in fact, saved her from certain injury, if not death, perhaps it would be safe to let her guard down. A little. Maybe even enjoy the only adventure she'd be likely to experience before she returned home and was forced into some loveless, miserable marriage.

Her rescuer sat close beside her and held out his raised arm, his plaid draped across it.

"Yer teeth are chattering so furiously I'm afraid they may crack," he said with a slight smile.

His eyebrow quirked up in question, and she nodded slowly. She should refuse, she knew. But her blood felt as though it were turning to ice. If he did mean her harm, at least she'd die warm.

He wrapped an arm about her shoulders, his plaid draped over both of them. She settled against him with a sigh. How a man could be so warm, she didn't know. He seemed to have a personal fire burning in his breast. She couldn't help but gravitate toward it. The heat from the fire and the warmth of the man beside her created quite comfortable surroundings, despite her damp clothing.

"I apologize for my forwardness," he said, holding her a bit closer.

She glanced up at him through her lashes, wondering what her best friend, Lady Alice Chivers, would be doing under similar circumstances. Probably charming him until he fell under her spell. A world-class flirt, Alice had made no secret of her admiration for the dashing highwayman. Elizabet, on the other hand, spent her time hiding from possible suitors, not trying to draw them in. Her flirtatious skills had withered and rusted from misuse. Not that she should be using them in such a situation, anyway.

"No apologies necessary, sir. It is thanks to my poor judgment you are stuck out here in the storm with a sodden lady and a grumpy horse." She nodded her head at the animal who blew an annoyed burst of breath at them.

The man laughed. "Nay, dinna worry on his account, my lady. He's a sullen old fool, to be sure, but he'll be set to rights soon enough. In the meantime, we are both at yer service."

"That's very gallant of you."

"Aye, it is," he said, sounding surprised.

That startled a laugh out of her and she slapped a hand over her mouth. But a sudden, burning sting had her hissing in pain.

The highwayman frowned in concern and took her hand in his. "Looks as though the reins have torn yer hand a bit. Did ye no' have gloves?"

"I did, but they must have fallen off."

He nodded. "It's no' so bad, though I'm sure it feels so." He jumped up and rummaged in his saddlebags, returning with a couple strips of linen and a waterskin.

Her eyes widened. "You do travel prepared, don't you?"

He shrugged. "Ye never ken when ye might be needing the odd bandage or two. It's always good to be prepared."

He took her hand and poured a bit of the cool water over the reddened stripe across her palm, then set to work gently dabbing it dry and wrapping it up. "Ye'll be wanting to get a bit of salve for that once ye get back to the manor."

Her gaze shot up, her heart pounding with a burst of unease. "How is it you know where I am staying?"

"Barrington Manor is the only house around here that might be host to one such as yerself," he said, making a small adjustment to the bandage on her hand. "Ye're far too grand a lady to be from any of the villages."

"Oh," she said, embarrassed at her fear and his assessment of her.

"There ye are." He patted her hand but didn't release it.

"Thank you," she said, leaving her hand where it was.

"My pleasure, my lady."

She stared up into his eyes, long enough that the world narrowed until nothing else remained. Warmth spread through her from where his hands gently held hers, and her corset suddenly felt too tight. She'd never been so affected by a man before. Whether due to the circumstances or merely *him*, she didn't know. Or care. She knew only that the man intrigued her. Despite the discomfort and possible danger, she found being in his company…exhilarating. Perhaps it would last a few hours longer.

Eventually, she would be missed, if she wasn't already. Certainly, the last thing she wanted was another lecture from her mother on the correct behavior expected from a lady. Or from her father on the importance of maintaining proper appearances at all times and how she would never find a husband to rescue the family from their impending doom. Her parents' approved list of pastimes did not include sitting cuddled up beside a notorious highwayman.

She should return before she caused more trouble. "I haven't seen any lightning in a while. I suppose it's safe enough to return now."

"Aye," he said, still staring deep into her eyes, her hand cradled in his. "I suppose it is."

But he didn't release her hand or make any move to stand. Instead, he wrapped his hand more firmly about hers, slowly drawing it to his chest, and her with it. He brushed a damp ringlet from her forehead.

"Forgive me, my lady," he murmured, "but I dinna believe I've ever seen a lass so beautiful as you. Ye've quite robbed me of my senses."

Heat rushed to her cheeks, and she fought to keep her wits about her. "I thought you were supposed to be robbing me."

"Aye. That's the usual way of it. Though ye dinna seem to have much in the way of valuables on ye. Perhaps I should steal a kiss instead."

He brushed a thumb across her lower lip and leaned in closer. Her heart pounded at the proximity of his lips.

The sound of horses coming through the trees gave them only seconds warning of visitors.

"Well, this is a cozy scene."

The highwayman jumped up and had a pistol in his hand aimed at the intruder before Elizabet could blink.

Fergus Ramsay, the man most likely to become her husband, unless she succeeded in talking her father out of it, calmly drew his sword. How in the world had he found her? She thought about ignoring him. Perhaps even doing something really shocking and wrapping her arms around the highlander to show Fergus that it wasn't *him* she desired. The temptation tore at her, urging her on. But the images of her parents' faces decided her. The looks of horror she already faced at being found in the innocent company of another man, let alone what she'd face at the discovery of the identity of her current company, were enough to keep her from acting.

She shook out her skirts, her movements unhurried. Fergus fumed quietly, his fury betrayed by the obvious set of his jaw, the hard, dark eyes that watched her every move, the white knuckles that squeezed the reins in his hand, the nervous shifting of his horse beneath him. His gaze flickered to her every few seconds, but he kept most of his focus on the man beside her.

She should probably be afraid. Do something to calm the situation. Assure Fergus that she wasn't harmed. That nothing had been exchanged between her and the highwayman but words.

But truthfully, she didn't care what Fergus thought of her. He didn't own her. Yet. Annoyance and disappointment coursed through her more than any other emotion. Her heroic, dangerous stranger had been seconds from kissing her. And now that the possibility no longer existed, she wanted his kiss more than anything she'd wanted in a long time.

Damn Fergus! He would probably be the bane of her life for a good many years. Why did he have to start so soon?

"Mr. Ramsay," she said, her voice as flat and emotionless as she could make it. "However did you find me?"

His eyes narrowed slightly. "My dear Elizabet, you speak as though you didn't want to be found."

She gave him a cold smile. "Not at all. I'm simply surprised you were able to, considering I'm not even sure where I am."

"Oh?" he said, his gaze moving to the highwayman. "You seem to be keeping strange company. Did this...*gentleman* spirit you away?"

"Of course not. The storm caught me by surprise, and my horse bolted. He rescued me."

"Rescued you? I didn't think highwaymen were in the business of rescuing fair maidens." Fergus looked her highwayman up and down, his scowl deepening. He gripped his sword tighter. "I suppose I should be grateful I found you before the ransom note arrived." He turned his attention back to the highwayman. "Or were you merely going to rob her of anything worth taking and then leave my betrothed to the wolves?"

"Not betrothed yet," Elizabet reminded him.

"Soon enough," he said, the steel in his voice brooking no argument.

The highwayman retook his place by her side, not touching her, but standing close enough to offer his support should she need it. He kept his weapon trained on Fergus. "I dinna believe ye answered the lady's question."

Fergus's expression turned thunderous, but to her surprise, he kept a tight rein on his anger. "Her horse returned without her. I was already saddled and ready to begin a search when the mare wandered back to the stables. I simply followed the direction from which she came. And a good thing I did. Who knows what sort of mischief might have befallen her?"

The highwayman gave him a tight, mirthless smile. "I would have kept her from harm. In fact, I planned to return her to the manor as soon as the rain let up."

"Oh? Planning to attack your victims in their own homes now?"

"Nay. My prey is carefully chosen. Men who deserve my wrath. Not innocent women and children huddling in their homes. That seems to be something you're more familiar with. Mr....Ramsay, is it?"

Fergus glared at him. "If you were any sort of gentleman, I'd call you out for such an insult. But as you are nothing more than a common criminal, I wouldn't bother to sully my blade with you. Elizabet," he said, turning to her. "Come."

Her eyes narrowed. *Come.* As if she were a dog under his heel.

"My lady," the highwayman said, his quiet voice for her alone. "If ye dinna wish to return with him, I'll see ye safely home."

His words sent her stomach careening about, and she wished nothing more than to take him up on his offer. But she already had enough trouble awaiting her. Fergus spoke the truth. He was her intended. Minus the official paperwork. For all intents and purposes, she'd be his bride in the near future. Angering him and her parents would only make her life worse.

She sighed. "Thank you. I appreciate the offer. However,

I should probably return with him."

He nodded, his face closed down, not revealing anything he might be feeling. He took her hand and brought it to his lips. "Thank you for a most diverting afternoon, my lady."

He lingered over her hand until Fergus snapped. "Elizabet. Your parents are waiting."

She sighed again, gathered her skirts in her hands, and flounced over to the horse held by one of the grooms who'd accompanied Fergus. Her highwayman chuckled quietly, and when she mounted and turned back to him, he gave her a jaunty little wave with the hand that didn't have a pistol trained on Fergus.

"Robert, escort Lady Elizabet back to the manor. I'll be along shortly."

Elizabet frowned and looked back, concern for her rescuer filling her. He winked, and the flirtatious gesture brought a smile back to her lips. She nodded her head at him and then turned her horse to follow the groom back to the manor.

She wasn't sure who her highwayman was or how he knew Fergus, but she wanted to find out everything about him.

Being scared out of her wits had never been so invigorating. She could almost hope to do it again.

Chapter Two

While John MacGregor wished nothing more than to accompany the delectable Elizabet back to Barrington Manor himself, he needed to find out what in the seven blazes of hell Fergus Campbell, or Ramsay as he appeared to be calling himself, was doing so far from his father's lands in Scotland. Or why he was so far from London, where he'd been sent after the skirmish at Glenlyon.

Fergus, it seemed, shared his eagerness. Fergus looked him up and down with a sneer that had John clenching his fists for control.

"Well, well. The Highland Highwayman." He spat the name out as though it left a foul taste upon his tongue. "I must admit I'd assumed the tales of your deeds were merely bedtime stories to amuse children. And yet, here you are. Quite far from your home, it would seem. I must admit, I find you…disappointing. I suppose most fantasies fail to live up to reality."

"Aye, as *yer* fantasies of assuming leadership of the Campbell clan never lived up to reality. I didna think to see ye again after the MacGregor Lion sent ye scampering back to yer mother after yer ill-advised campaign."

Fergus's eyes narrowed to slits. "You give yourself away. You must be one of Malcolm MacGregor's lapdogs. Only a MacGregor would believe the lies he has spread of our little skirmish. And his prowess. A failure I shall remedy the next time we meet."

"I'm sure he looks forward to that day, Campbell."

Fergus's expression darkened, and John couldn't keep a satisfied smile from his lips. "My apologies," John said, though his tone betrayed no such remorse. "Ramsay now, is it?"

"My mother's name, and the only one I claim."

John raised an eyebrow. "I'm sure yer father might disagree…"

"I have no father," Fergus spat. "A man who would betray his only son, turn him in like some criminal—"

"Ye *are* a criminal," John said, raising the pistol a bit. "What else do ye call waging war on a neighboring clan against the orders of yer father and chief?"

"I did what my father was too weak to do. I kept our clan safe, made it strong."

"You ransacked villages with no cause, maimed and killed innocents, stole or destroyed crops and livestock, and devastated countless lives. And were sent to London for appropriate punishment. Which, I see, ye managed to weasel yer way out of."

"And how do you know so much about it?"

"I keep my eyes open and my ears to the ground. The charges against ye were grievous."

Fergus gave him a sneering smile. "It helps to have sponsors who will vouch for you. Oh, you needn't worry. I spent a few weeks languishing in that hellhole they call a prison. But, as I said, the word of a few well-placed men who know the right people goes a long way."

"And where did ye get the money to buy yerself such support? I know yer father wouldna have helped ye."

"How would you know anything about my father? Have you switched loyalties? Abandoned your MacGregor master for a Campbell? I suppose it matters little. Sending a masked coward to prance about the forests at night would be a likely thing for either of them to do."

John's grip tightened on his pistol, his finger itching to pull the trigger.

"I dinna work for anyone. But I make it my business to ken what is going on."

"Yes, well isn't it fortunate to have two parents? The inheritance from my *English* mother bought my freedom and will buy me a highborn English wife. And I'll use her to breed the Scottish taint from my blood once and for all."

The thought of Fergus laying one hand on Elizabet filled John with a rage so strong it soured his stomach. He pulled a second pistol from his belt and leveled them both at Fergus.

"Get off yer horse before I shoot him out from under ye."

Fergus cocked a brow.

"Willing to fight a duel for a bit of skirt you don't even know? I didn't realize you were so foolhardy. I'm one of the best swordsmen in the country."

"Maybe so, but that is relevant only if I were intending to use a sword. Or fight a duel. Which I'm not. I'm merely giving ye the opportunity to die on yer feet. Now, get down," he said, giving each pistol a little shake.

Before Fergus could answer, the sound of another horse approaching filtered through the trees, and both men stopped to see who approached.

Philip, John's friend, distant cousin, and right-hand man slowly entered the clearing.

He reined in his horse and took in the scene before

him, his masked eyes glancing at John for silent orders. His appearance returned some semblance of sanity to John, though he gripped the pistols so tightly his joints ached. While he'd love nothing more than to ensure Fergus never left that clearing, it would solve nothing. Well, actually it would solve a great deal. But it would also cause more complications than John had the time or desire to deal with. He finally gave a slight shake of his head and stifled a sigh.

Fergus briefly glanced at Philip, his face twisting in a grimace before turning back to John. "We will have to settle this another time. I must return to the manor. Elizabet's father and I still have a few points to finalize. And I'm suddenly very eager to claim my bride."

His lecherous smile had John taking a step toward him, his guns raised again. Philip moved his horse closer, keeping his distance, though obviously ready to intervene, if needed.

"If I were you, ye wee bastard, I'd be sure never to cross my path again," John said.

Fergus didn't even bat an eye. "You're awfully eager to see my blood spilled. Not that I care one wit about your pathetic vendetta. But I am curious as to what has spurred such an ungodly hatred."

John's chest heaved with the effort it took not to kill the piece of human filth before him. "I have vowed to avenge my brother's death. I'll not rest until you are in the ground with him."

Ramsay's eyebrows rose at that. "Oh? Did I kill him?" he said, his tone as happily casual as if he were asking if he might have another cake at tea.

John's finger itched to squeeze the trigger. "He was a soldier, killed while attempting to apprehend a band of smugglers."

Ramsay shook his head with a *tsk*ing sound. "Such dangerous times in which we live." He smiled down at John.

"My condolences to your family."

"Ye filthy, murdering bastard!" John lunged, but Philip moved his horse to block him.

Ramsay glared at him. "What makes you think I had anything to do with the death of some obscure soldier on a godforsaken moor?"

John smiled, though he knew the expression was as cold as the ice running through his veins. "There have been rumors about your involvement. And as I never said *where* my brother was killed, I'd say you just confirmed those suspicions."

Ramsay's face paled, but he maintained his arrogant attitude. "I'm sure the word of a highwayman will hold up nicely in court," he said, his smug smile turning John's stomach.

John swore and took aim over Philip's horse, but Fergus laughed and wheeled his horse about, disappearing into the trees before John could say anything else.

John rounded on Philip. "Why did ye stop me? He killed Angus! He all but admitted it."

Philip dismounted. "Maybe so. Or maybe he was merely trying to rile ye into a temper. Either way, there's naught ye can do about it now. Killin' him would have brought ye more trouble than ye need."

John shoved his pistols back into their holsters, his lungs burning as though he'd run ten miles. The death of his brother still festered, raw and unforgiving. Having Fergus throw it in his face was a bitter pill to swallow.

"What was Fergus Campbell doing here?" Philip asked.

"Fergus Ramsay, he's callin' himself now," John all but spit out. "I'm no' sure what his plans are, but I dinna think he's up to any good." He tore his eyes from the spot where Fergus had disappeared into the trees and looked at Philip. "How did ye find me?"

"I was watching the manor as ye asked. As far as I can tell, Lord Dawsey is planning on leaving in the morning, so I've sent word to the men to ready themselves for daybreak."

John nodded his agreement and waited for Philip to continue.

"There was a great uproar when the girl's horse turned up without her. I saw Fergus and recognized him. Thought I'd follow and see if I could discover what the wee bastard was doing here. And found you."

John rammed his hand through his hair and kicked some dirt over the fire before mounting his own horse. "He's up to no good. He'll bear some watching."

Philip regarded him until John nearly squirmed under his gaze. "What is it, man?"

Philip shrugged. "Ye think he had something to do with what happened to Angus?"

"How else would he know of the death of an obscure soldier? If he wasna standing on that moor with the smugglers, he wasna far away."

"So, this is about yer brother then? Not about this girl?"

John was about to argue, but Philip wouldn't believe him anyway. "Not entirely, but aye, I'd pity any woman bound to that bastard."

"Aye," Philip agreed. "But there's no law against it, John. Like it or not, she's not our concern. Ye need to keep yer distance. Or all our plans will be for naught."

John clenched his jaw until his teeth ached, and he wheeled his horse around without answering. Philip was right. He couldn't risk everything they'd worked toward because he had taken a passing fancy to some girl. And while he was certain Fergus knew more about his brother than he'd said, he was also certain Fergus wasn't the man in charge of the operation. As much as he ached to slide a blade between Fergus's ribs, he might be their best chance at taking down the bigger game.

Besides, he might be able to spear two rabbits with one arrow and prevent Fergus from marrying Elizabet by taking Fergus himself down. Whatever he was doing in England, John was sure he was up to no good.

Discover that, and he could bring Fergus the justice he richly deserved, avenge his brother, and save Elizabet from a life of misery.

. . .

Elizabet leaned back against the cushions of the carriage bench, her head pounding with frustration. After a token exclamation of concern at her adventure of the day, her parents had spent the better part of the afternoon berating her for risking the match with Fergus Ramsay. The only match likely for her now that her reputation was jeopardized, and that was if he'd still have her. Servants talked. By the time they reached London, half the town would likely know she'd been found in intimate circumstances with an outlawed highwayman.

She seriously doubted anyone in London would care, as most of them had done far worse. Then again, most had the wherewithal not to get caught. And the fact that the man was a notorious criminal didn't do her any favors. Had he been anyone else, her transgression would hardly have made a ripple.

Under the circumstances, her parents had thought it best to promptly pack their bags and head back to London, despite the doctor's advice for Elizabet to rest for the night and postpone journeying until the next day, at least. They'd bundled her into the carriage before they'd had a chance to digest their dinner, hoping to beat the gossip to town.

"Father," she finally said, interrupting yet another tirade.

"I know Mr. Ramsay is wealthy and that his money could help the family. But we don't even know where his wealth comes from. We know nothing about him, really. Shouldn't we find out before…"

"That is none of your concern, young lady!" Her father threw up his hands and sat back against his seat, glancing at her mother for validation. "Honestly, listen to the cheek of the girl. Pretending to know anything of the situation. Acting as though she knows best."

"But Father, he could be a criminal, or…"

He turned his attention back to Elizabet. "Judging by what happened today, you can hardly complain about that! You seem to have no trouble with criminals. I do not care where his wealth comes from. I care only that he's willing to spend it to get himself a wife. Your only dowry is some run-down estates from your grandmother. All you have is that pretty face and a good family name to entice a husband. We are not going to turn down the one man who is willing to take you with little incentive *and* is willing to pay for the honor. We must pray he still wants to do so after this incident."

"I didn't do anything wrong, Father. Except nearly get myself killed in the storm."

"I'll not discuss it any further!"

"But don't you find it odd that the man was born in Scotland but speaks without a hint of an accent? Or that no one knows why he was sent from home in disgrace, or if he even was, for that matter? That is my point exactly. No one seems to know anything about him. At all. You don't find that concerning?"

"I don't care what occurred in his past or what youthful indiscretions got him sent away from Scotland. Godforsaken place, anyway. Why anyone would choose to live there, I can't imagine. I care only that he does not change his mind about the future. You very nearly ruined us all!"

He turned back to her mother. "Imagine the insolence, riding out against our wishes. Getting caught in that storm. Being found in the arms of some outlaw in the middle of the woods."

Elizabet started to argue that point again but realized that, strictly speaking, it was true. Still… "Father, I've told you, nothing happened. He rescued me, found shelter, tried to keep us warm. That is it. When you say it like that, it sounds so much worse than what actually occurred."

"Yes, that is the problem. It doesn't matter what really happened, only what people will *say* happened. Mr. Ramsay was certainly too much of a gentleman to mention it, but servants talk, Elizabet. Don't ever forget that. I bet half the county knows of your little tête-à-tête by now. We can only hope the gossip doesn't ruin everything!"

Elizabet turned to look out the window and choked back the lump in her throat. Her father would never see reason. How could he auction off his only child to the highest bidder? She'd never understand. Nor would she ever do such a thing to her own children, should she have any. With Fergus. Though handsome enough, his cold demeanor overshadowed his pleasing features. He never acted overtly cruel, but something about him unsettled her. The thought of being married to him sent a cold shiver up her spine. She, however, had no say in the matter, even though she would never love him.

She repressed a shudder.

"Do stop pouting, dear," her mother said. "You'll get frown lines."

Elizabet bit her lip and kept her gaze firmly out the window, though she couldn't see much in the night. The moonlight illuminated some of the landscape, but not a great deal. The lanterns swinging from the carriage cast ominous shadows on their surroundings. Or maybe that only reflected her mood.

The exhaustion of being the Earl of Dawsey's daughter always pulled at her. Always aware that she must live up to the reputation her father had worked so hard to cultivate. That of a prosperous lord in great favor with the king. A pretense, in point of fact, but one that must be maintained at all times. Her father lived in deathly fear of his peers discovering how precarious his position was, both at court and with his creditors.

As a lord who'd supported the former Lord Protector of the Commonwealth of England, Scotland, and Ireland, Oliver Cromwell, Lord Dawsey had navigated an almost impressive road back to favor, or tolerance more like, once King Charles II had regained his throne. Elizabet was fairly certain the only reason her father hadn't ended up swinging from a rope at Tyburn was because the king simply didn't have the time or resources to exact retribution from all the traitorous subjects who had deserved it. The most prominent ones had been punished, naturally. Her father had never been prominent, though, no matter who ran the kingdom. A fact which beleaguered him, but had probably saved his neck.

And now, furthering his ambitions claimed all his attention. As his only child, an attractive daughter of marriageable age, Elizabet's value as his most prized possession lay in what she could bring him through her marriage.

She tried to put everything out of her mind. Everything but the charismatic man who'd rescued her in the forest. She would think of *him* for the rest of her days, regretting only that they hadn't had more time together. She'd have liked to have had a kiss to remember through the cold, lonely years married to a man like Fergus Ramsay.

She closed her eyes and sighed.

Chapter Three

John kept a tight rein on his anxious horse, wishing it were as easy to keep a rein on anxious men. The sudden change in plans didn't sit well with his crew, though they were well enough trained, for the most part, to adapt quickly. Luckily, Philip had thought to leave a scout at the manor to keep an eye on things, or they'd have met at the rendezvous point at dawn to discover their prey had escaped in the night.

Will, the newest member of the Highland Highwayman's crew, fidgeted at John's side, his hand edging toward his pistol. John frowned, his gaze flicking toward Philip, who nodded and eased his horse closer to Will.

"Keep yer hand off yer weapon unless ye intend to use it, Will. We dinna want any mistakes tonight. No one is to be harmed."

"Oh, yes sir, I know. My apologies."

Philip and John shared another look, Philip giving him a slight shrug. Will was a good man, generally handy to have around, but young and much too highly strung for John's liking. The last thing they needed was a dead body to deal with. It *was* the first job they'd allowed him to ride. Hopefully, with a bit more experience he'd calm.

John might be a highwayman during his nocturnal hours, but he still had some principles. He and his men swept in, took whatever easily disposable goodies the corrupt and traitorous noblemen had handy, and rode on. They might leave their prey angry and slightly less wealthy, but they always left them alive and, whenever possible, uninjured. John wanted to keep it that way. The price on his head, well, on the Highland Highwayman's head, would go a whole lot higher if he accumulated a body count. He desired to right the wrongs committed under Oliver Cromwell. Not commit more atrocities.

The eerie call of an owl sounded from the direction of the woods. His lookout's signal.

"Get into position," John said, sending Will and Philip into the tree line.

A few more minutes...

The distant rumble of wheels echoed through the night, and John jerked his head toward the road dimly lit in the moonlight below him. The carriage ambled along at a slow, steady pace, heading straight for the narrow, wooded passage where his men waited.

A thrill shot through John. He didn't necessarily enjoy this pastime of his—or at least not all aspects of it—but he couldn't deny that it did liven things up a bit. And he did enjoy knocking a few corrupt nobles from their ivory perches. They might be his peers by birth, but most certainly not by honor. They didn't know the meaning of the word. John relished enlightening them.

The carriage entered the passage, and John spurred his horse into action, thundering down the embankment and drawing even with the coach as his men burst from the trees. The carriage's team reared in surprise. Feminine shrieks emanated from inside, along with a stream of profanity from a more masculine throat.

John frowned. There shouldn't be any women in the carriage. It belonged to Thomas Harding, the Earl of Dawsey, an arrogant blowhard who liked to overtax his starving tenants and whose dealings under Cromwell, and in recent years, should rightly have the man swinging from a rope. John also highly suspected it was Dawsey who was behind the smuggling ring that had gotten his brother killed, but he hadn't been able to gather enough evidence. Fergus's reappearance at the same country house where Dawsey had been staying served only to strengthen John's suspicions that Fergus was also involved. John wouldn't rest until the smuggling operation had been taken down, and the men in charge, in chains. And if one of those men happened to be Fergus, that would make it all the sweeter.

In the meantime, he would make Dawsey's life as miserable as possible. Like a cat toying with his prey. Dawsey's actions had caused the misery of many, and most likely the death of Angus. He deserved every ounce of retribution John could lay at his feet.

John looked at Philip who shrugged. Lord Dawsey should be traveling back to court while his wife and daughter remained behind at the Barrington's. Apparently, they'd changed their minds. Which made that night's work more delicate than John would have liked. Women had a tendency to ruin even the best-laid plans. No help for it, though.

Will kept his gun trained on the driver while Philip's gun joined John's, pointing at the carriage door and the agitated occupants inside. John yanked open the door to reveal a middle-aged couple squawking with indignation. And a young woman, most likely their daughter. A connection he cursed himself for not making sooner.

Elizabet sat staring at him with an intense mixture of

curiosity and excitement. In the dark of night he knew she couldn't be sure he was the same highwayman who'd rescued her earlier that day. Though surely the coincidence would be hard to ignore. However, even if she recognized him, he wasn't flirting with her in the firelight, but robbing her coach at gunpoint. So she should be afraid. Yet, if she felt fear, she didn't let it show. How refreshing. Would that her mother could follow suit. His ears would be ringing for a week.

He let a smile touch his lips and held out his hand to Elizabet. "My apologies, lass. But I'm afraid I'll have to ask ye to step down."

She didn't hesitate, but slid her hand into his. Her quickness made him pause...did she know him, after all? Then she lurched out of the carriage, throwing herself on him with a shout. He caught the glint of metal in the moonlight in time to twist out of the line of danger. She stumbled over her skirts and he lunged to catch her, though he took care to stay out of reach of her dagger.

He twisted her arm behind her, wrenching the blade from her hand. The tip easily pierced his thumb when tested. It was sharp. And she knew how to use it.

"Impressive," he said.

She brushed her hands down her skirts, setting everything to rights. "Thank you," she said, her voice tight with anger. "Now if you don't mind." She held out her hand.

He laughed and tucked it into his belt. "Nay, lass. I think I'll hold onto this for now."

She glared at him and crossed her arms. "You have no right to hold us here. And most certainly no right to steal our property. You have no shame, sir! Rest assured, the king himself will hear of this!"

"Och, of that I have nay doubt, my lady. However, by the time His Majesty has heard the tale of my wickedness, I'll be long gone and nothing but a pleasant dream."

"Nightmare is more like it. You are a scoundrel, sir."

He chuckled. "I've been called worse, my lady. Far worse."

"But I doubt you've been called better."

He merely grinned. "And by ladies far less beautiful than you."

Her eyes locked with his, their dark depths, the color of a new fawn's coat in the sunlight, now deepened to a dark amber in the night. They sucked him in, making him feel naked, exposed, as though she'd suddenly stripped him of the mask he wore. He resisted the urge to squirm under her scrutiny.

"I suppose pretty speeches like that are why tales abound of your gallantry."

He swept a bow, though he kept his gaze firmly on her. She wasn't one to let his guard down around. For more than one reason. "I'm glad ye approve."

She gave a most unladylike snort and shook her head. "I didn't say I approved. Pretty enough words, but spoken by a man such as yourself, in a situation such as this, and any woman would have to be daft to think you meant anything by them. I confess, I found you much more charming when you weren't holding my family at the end of your pistol."

John laughed again. Oh, she was even more amusing spoiling for a fight than she was wet and bedraggled in the woods. He wished he could linger. He wouldn't mind matching wits with her. It wasn't often he came across someone who could surprise him. Her parents, on the other hand… While neither he nor the delightful woman by his side had paid any attention to the continued threats and exhortations from them while they'd sized each other up, her parents' shrieks for justice grew harder to ignore. Philip would maim him for certain for leaving him to deal with the fools.

John winced at a few high-pitched screams from the now

hysterical Lady Dawsey.

"Madam," he said, raising his voice above the din. "If ye willna keep quiet, I'll have ye gagged."

She hiccupped to a stop, pressing one hand to her great, heaving bosom, and fanning her face with the other.

"And if ye faint, I'll let ye lie in the road until our business is concluded."

Her constitution instantly improved, though a few whimpers escaped every so often.

He turned back to Elizabet. "My apologies, my lady. As ye so succinctly pointed out, I prefer not to treat ladies so harshly but…"

Her gaze flicked to her mother and back to him and she turned her head so her mother could not see her face. "It's quite all right. There are times I wish I could get away with that threat myself."

John snorted, barely managing to contain a laugh. "Indeed," he muttered.

He couldn't imagine being the child of such parents, who seemed far more concerned about the safety of the jewels they were hastily trying to hide rather than the safety of their daughter as she stood in close proximity to the man who'd seized their carriage. He shook his head as Lord Dawsey's large ruby ring disappeared into his wife's bodice.

John held out his hand to Elizabet and, after a brief hesitation, she took it.

He looked her over, his eyes roving from her voluminous skirts to the tightly corseted torso that displayed her breasts so magnificently. "Ye wouldna be hiding any other sharp objects in there, would ye?"

A smile tugged at her lips. "I wouldn't tell you if I did."

"Feisty wee thing, aren't ye? I suppose I'll have to keep a close eye on ye."

She shrugged, a gentle movement of her shoulders that

caused the soft lace spilling from her bodice to shift slightly. He tore his gaze away from the expanse of creamy skin the dress exposed. Her cloak had come untied in their scuffle and fallen to the ground.

He bent to retrieve it and held it out. She looked at him in surprise.

"I dinna wish for ye to take a chill."

She didn't come to him immediately, and he waited, as he had earlier that day, until she decided he could be trusted. At least far enough to provide her some warmth. She finally blew out an irritated breath, though he wasn't sure if the annoyance was aimed at him or herself, and turned her back so he could drape the heavy fabric across her shoulders.

"Thank you," she muttered, obviously galled to be obliged to him.

He drew the cloak tight about her, savoring the feel of her soft, supple body in his arms before she wrenched away from him.

She tied the ribbons at her neck and wrapped herself in the material, perusing him the way he'd done to her.

"You're the Highland Highwayman," she said, before he had the chance to utter another word.

His eyebrow rose. "Not verra hard to come to that conclusion, now is it, lass? I'm surprised ye didna ask the last time we met."

Her head cocked to the side as she studied him, sending the blond ringlets gathered above each ear swinging. "I thought it might be rude to mention the fact when you'd risked yourself to rescue me. As you are now the one I need to be rescued from, I have no such qualms."

He barked out a laugh again. Oh, he'd never enjoyed himself so much on a robbery. She definitely made the job much more entertaining.

"I've always wondered why a Scotsman would travel so

far from home to do his wicked deeds," she said. "We are near the border, I suppose. Still, a bit out of the way for you, I'd think."

"I have my reasons. Curious wee thing, aren't ye?"

"No harm in that," she said, giving him a sweet smile that had probably worked wonders in weaseling trifles and baubles from a court full of fawning men.

"On the contrary, lass, curiosity, especially about matters that dinna concern ye, can be a dangerous thing indeed."

Her smile faded a bit around the edges, her eyes finally tinged with a speck of fear. He didn't wish to frighten her—at least not too much—but it certainly wouldn't do her any harm to practice a bit more caution. Especially in the dark of night when surrounded by men with guns and swords.

"I believe it very much concerns me, since you've decided to hold my family hostage, no doubt to reap whatever treasures you can from us." She jutted her pert little nose in the air, daring him to contradict her.

"Point taken, lass. Perhaps I'll tell ye my tale sometime."

"I have no wish to hear it."

Judging by her apparently curious nature and her fidgeting as she answered, he doubted that. But it would be rude to point it out. "As ye wish," he said, tipping his hat to her.

He turned his attention back to the coach and her parents, who had finally subsided on the side of the road in a heap of finery and dire mutterings. Time to focus on what he was here to do.

"If ye'll pardon me, my lady," he said.

It took him only moments to locate the hollow space beneath the carriage's bench where Lord Dawsey had stashed part of his once considerable fortune. He pulled out four leather sacks, each about the size of a loaf of bread, from the depths beneath the bench. Elizabet's eyes grew wide.

"I'll wager ye werena aware of yer father's penchant for traveling with a large portion of his wealth?"

She shook her head and stepped closer. She frowned. "Seems a foolish thing to do," she muttered.

John snorted again. "Aye, it is. And too much of a temptation for a man of such low morals as myself. Though describing the money as *his* isna completely accurate."

Her frown deepened. "What do you mean by that?"

"Have ye never considered where yer wealth originated?" He didn't give her a chance to answer. "No…of course not."

Anger mixed with the confusion on the girl's face. "According to my father, we have no wealth."

He snorted again. "As ye can see, that isna quite the truth. Though I reckon it's a far bit less than it once was."

"I didn't realize…"

"I meant no insult, my lady," he assured her. "It is hardly something ye'd need to worry about, after all."

She ignored that comment. "Explain what you meant."

John took a deep breath. He had neither the time nor the desire to enlighten Elizabet as to the nature of her odious father and his many misdeeds.

"Explain," she demanded again. "Is this…is this all from his tenants?"

His eyes widened behind his mask. Imperious little thing, wasn't she? Though not so little, really. She was unfashionably tall for a woman, her head reaching to just beneath his chin. Most women were no taller than his chest. Her long willowy limbs looked strong, though, and the amply rounded breasts barely contained by her gown promised sweet, soft curves beneath the many layers of fabric she wore. Curves he'd had only a mere taste of and couldn't erase from his mind.

She folded her arms across her richly embroidered bodice, the jewelry on her wrists and fingers glinting in the moonlight. She waited for his answer with barely restrained impatience.

John gathered the bags and motioned for her to follow.

"Some of it, aye. But much of it is from those he had no legal right to take from. As despicable a landlord as yer father is, he unfortunately has the right to tax his tenants as he sees fit. However, much of his wealth yer father gained during Cromwell's ill-gotten reign, bleeding his royalist neighbors dry. And, ever the opportunist, he switched sides in time for His Majesty King Charles's triumphant return."

She shook her head, her eyes wide with horror. John pitied her, but pressed on.

"Before His Majesty's return, however, yer father seems to have tried his hand at smuggling. Now, I could look past that. Cromwell denied the people a great many things, and I've no grudge against a man making a bit of coin providing goods that canna be gotten any other way. But under yer father's operation, men got hurt. Innocent men. And that I willna abide."

He stopped and cleared his throat, the memory of his once laughing, adventurous brother lying dead in the dust too much to bear. He didn't know why he felt it so important to make her understand that what he did had purpose. But he pressed on anyway.

"Since His Majesty's return, yer father has taken to inflating his coffers the good old-fashioned way...by leeching it from tenants who can ill afford to pay and are forced to do so, anyway. Whether he still does the odd night of smuggling remains to be seen. And, of course, the bribes and blackmailed funds from his old cronies from Cromwell's days who didna have the foresight to change allegiance before the king returned—and who are willing to pay handsomely to keep their shortcomings from the king's attention."

"He wouldn't," she murmured.

"I'm sorry to inform ye, lass, he has. This money doesna

belong to him."

She glared at him. "Neither does it belong to you. You, it seems, are no better than he."

"On the contrary, my lady. I'm a great deal better."

He left it at that. Yes, he kept a decent portion for himself and his men. His clan had suffered terribly, not only under Cromwell but under many English kings, until Charles had retaken the throne. So John had few qualms about exacting a little retribution from those he knew had made his kinsmen's lot worse. But he shared the majority of the wealth he stole. Whether by anonymously settling accounts or leaving a few coins in the chicken coop, he did what he could to ease the way of those villagers and merchants who'd suffered before the king had regained his throne.

But he had no desire to explain that to his young captive. He was out of time. And he'd already spent far too much time explaining who he was, and why he did what he did, to his enemy's daughter. Not the wisest course of action.

The bags clinked when he passed them to Philip, who stored them quickly in his saddlebags. Lord Dawsey shouted incoherently, his mottled cheeks purple with rage.

"You...you bastard! Brigand! You'll steal my entire fortune and leave me destitute in the street?"

John kept a tight rein on the fury that rushed through him. He stepped closer to the blustering fool, looming over him. "Come now, my lord. Ye did worse to a great many who trusted ye. And I'm quite certain ye've at least one more carriage such as this, full of yer stolen gains. I doubt ye'll even feel the loss. In fact, I quite hope we meet again one dark night. I'd be happy to relieve ye of more of yer worldly goods."

His eyes rested on Elizabet once again, roaming from bejeweled head to slippered foot and back again. Her beauty rivaled the moon itself. She sucked in an outraged breath, though whether her anger stemmed from his implication of her status as part of her father's worldly goods or his frank perusal of her, he didn't know. Either way, she returned his gaze boldly, drawing herself up to her full stature, as if preparing for battle.

He grinned, speaking while the idea still formed itself in his mind. He addressed the cursing Lord Dawsey again, though he kept his gaze on Elizabet. "In the spirit of fairness, to show ye what a generous man I can be, I'll return one of these bags to ye."

"Only one? What of the others? You can't simply—"

John held up his hand. "I can, and I shall, and if ye insist on being rude, I'll leave now with all four bags firmly in my possession."

Dawsey subsided with a huff, his cheeks growing so dark John feared he might expire on the spot. *Better hurry this along.*

"As I was saying, I will return one bag to ye. In exchange for a kiss," he said to the bewildered Elizabet who watched him with those glacial eyes.

Her jaw dropped. Her mother resumed her wailing. And her father didn't even hesitate.

"Done."

Chapter Four

Lord Dawsey shoved Elizabet at John before she could utter a protest. He caught her easily and held her stiff form in his arms. Anger on her behalf filled him to the brim. Yes, he'd asked for the kiss. But he'd done so on a whim, almost as a jest. To torment the apoplectic old toad. He'd never expected the man to turn over his own daughter so quickly for so little. For all he'd known, John had meant to snatch her and carry her away.

She held herself aloof, unresisting, but the rage permeating her easily eclipsed his own.

"My lady," he said softly.

She looked into his eyes, unwavering, unafraid. "Your actions suggest you see me as otherwise, sir," she answered with steel in her voice. "If you have no intention of treating me as a lady, you needn't continue to address me as such."

"You are every inch a lady." He brought her hand to his lips, lingering over the soft skin. He'd have liked nothing more than to taste those sweet, full lips of hers. But he would not do so under such circumstances. The tension in her body eased slightly and, with a final squeeze of her hand, he released her.

She remained where she was, looking at him with her forehead creased in confusion.

"Sir?" Philip said, his voice level, though John knew him well enough to detect a note of caution and concern. They'd already tarried far too long.

"The rope," John said.

Will dismounted and grasped Lord Dawsey, binding his hands behind his rather ample back. The driver was similarly trussed. Will glanced at the women, but John shook his head. They were no threat to him. Well, Elizabet would shove a dagger down his gullet, if given enough provocation, no doubt. But he had yet to leave a lady tied and helpless in the middle of the road, and he had no intention of starting with her.

He removed one of the sacks of gold from Philip's saddlebag and handed it to Elizabet.

She frowned. "But you've received no kiss, sir."

"Be quiet, you insolent little fool!" her father shouted.

She blanched and at a nod from John, Philip shoved a handkerchief into the man's mouth and bundled him back into the carriage. Lady Dawsey followed, taking the sack from Elizabet and casting concerned glances back and forth between her husband and daughter before climbing inside.

John turned back to Elizabet and drew a finger down her cheek. "A kiss from such a lady would be worth more money than I have to give. And I am no' such a blackguard as to force myself on an unwilling woman. I would be honored to kiss ye. In truth, 'tis taking considerable restraint to refrain from tasting these sweet lips."

She sucked in a startled breath as his thumb caressed her bottom lip.

He let his hand fall away, cursing his good intentions. "But I willna kiss ye until ye ask me to."

She gaped at him, her eyes like rippling pools of water in the light of the moon. He half hoped she'd ask him right then. Instead, she took a step back. Not a surprise, though disturbingly disappointing, nonetheless.

"Sir," Philip prompted again.

John nodded and mounted his horse. "Ye may release the men once we are out of sight," he said to Elizabet. "Until we meet again, my lady," he said, tipping his hat to her.

He had no idea why he'd said such a thing to her. He'd certainly never see her again. Not under the same circumstances, in any case. But for the first time in ages, he wished differently.

Elizabet reached for the door of the carriage, but she lingered, pausing to look back at him. Something caught her gaze, and she turned. Her dagger lay near a small bush, gleaming in the moonlight. She bent to retrieve it, straightening with it in her hand.

"Blade!" Will yelled, drawing his pistol.

John and Philip shouted, but Will's finger had already tightened on the trigger. A shot rang out.

And Elizabet fell.

. . .

The coach horses reared and bolted, taking with them the carriage containing her parents. They were out of sight within moments. Elizabet lay motionless on the ground, struggling to maintain consciousness. One of the men shouted at the one who'd shot her, jerking the gun from his hand. The bastard didn't put up a fight. Good. At least she didn't have to worry about getting shot again. He merely stared at her mumbling, "She had a blade," over and over.

"Wasn't going to use it, idiot," she murmured, though she couldn't be sure she'd even uttered it aloud, as it didn't register in her own ears.

The Highland Highwayman ignored him and rushed to her. She wished she knew his actual name. Saying The Highland Highwayman took a bit of effort. Not that she'd be saying it much. Even thinking it took more energy than she had. It occurred to her she might be rambling. Her thoughts, that is. Also, she didn't feel much pain. She'd been shot. Shouldn't it hurt?

The highwayman dropped to his knees by her side. He laid his fingers on the pulse at her neck.

That felt nice. Soft and tender.

"Faint, but steady," he said.

"I like your voice," she murmured.

He gave her a wry smile and laid his hand on her cheek. "Lie still, lass."

He pulled aside layers of velvet and lace until he located the wound.

"Am I dying?" she whispered, strangely not all that curious about the answer. Shouldn't she be? Seemed like something that should matter to her.

"Nay. The bullet pierced yer upper arm. A clean shot. All the way through." He breathed a sigh of relief. "I willna have to dig for it, at least."

"That's good," she said, her voice faint and slurred to her ears.

"That's verra good."

"Sir," one of the men said. The one who hadn't shot her. "We must go."

The highwayman nodded. "Aye." He swept his cloak off his shoulders and wrapped it about her. "Hold tight, love. I'll try not to jostle ye too much."

Before she could respond, he scooped her into his arms. She thought the other man protested. But they kept moving so her highwayman must not have agreed. She didn't remember much after he got her on the horse and climbed up behind her. He kept her tight against his chest. He emanated warmth. His solid arms encircling her offered safety. She'd been shot and now was being carried off to who-knew-where by a highwayman whose henchman was responsible. She should be terrified. Screaming. Calling for help.

Instead, she slumped back against him, sighed when his arm drew her closer, and drifted away.

The next several hours were a blur. The occasional jarring of her shoulder would jerk her awake periodically, sending white-hot pain shooting through her arm. At some point they stopped, and she felt herself being lifted from the horse. Carried inside. Someplace warm.

Something soft beneath her.

She sighed and burrowed deep into pillows beneath her head. And gave in to the darkness that pulled at her.

. . .

Warm sunlight filtered over Elizabet's face, and she carefully cracked open an eye. Her whole body ached. She closed her eyes and shifted, trying to find a comfortable spot. The jolt of pain burning through her shoulder had her instantly awake and gasping.

"Lie still," a deep voice said.

She turned her head, her eyes watering. "Where am I?" Her voice rasped, and a man came into view and handed her a cup.

"Water," he said. "Drink."

She frowned at him, recognizing her highwayman. She could hardly help but recognize him. He still wore his mask.

She took a deep drink and handed the cup back to him. "Wear that everywhere, do you?" she asked.

He grinned and reached for a pitcher on the table beside

the bed to refill her cup.

"Usually, no."

She accepted the cup gratefully. "Don't be shy on my account."

"I wear the mask for yer protection."

She drank and handed the cup back to him. "Don't you mean for yours?"

"Nay." He placed the cup on the table and grabbed a folded rag. "If you were to know my true identity, I'm afraid I'd have to…make sure the information went no further."

Elizabet didn't think he was jesting. She also didn't think he referred to a stern talking-to. He sat beside her and reached for her chemise. She drew away from him, and he frowned.

"I'm no' going to hurt ye. I need to check the bandage on yer shoulder," he said, his forehead creasing, as though he were somehow offended that she might think him a threat.

"Well, you did threaten to kill me if I saw your face. Not to mention it was your man who shot me. You can understand my caution."

His lips quirked up. "Indeed. It is always wise to be cautious."

"Where is my gown? I'll admit I don't remember much of the past several hours, but I am quite certain I was wearing one earlier this evening."

He chuckled. "It is over in the armoire, safe and sound. I thought ye'd rest more comfortably without it. And I didna wish to soil it while seeing to your wound."

He tended her shoulder with surprising gentleness, cleaning the wound and re-bandaging it with skill and speed.

"Bandage many gunshot wounds, do you?" she asked.

"A few."

He responded without an ounce of humor in his voice, and Elizabet was reminded what this man did for a living.

"Not that I'm not grateful, but why am I here?" she asked.

An eyebrow peeked up above the edge of the mask. "The horses bolted, taking yer carriage and yer parents off into the night, leaving ye quite alone. You'd rather I left ye in the dust to die?"

"No." She grimaced. "Horses must not like me much. They are always bolting and leaving me in dire straits. I had to be rescued last time, too."

"Well, perhaps I'm bad luck, as I happened to be in the vicinity both times."

She gave a delicate snort. "That's better than blaming my own shortcomings, I suppose."

"Always happy to be of service, my lady," he said with a smile.

She shivered and reached for the blanket but the movement sent another bolt of fire down her arm, and she drew in her breath with a hiss. He stood up long enough to pull the thick quilt up to her neck and then sat back beside her.

"Thank you," she said with a sigh. "No. I'm glad you didn't leave me to die. I suppose I simply don't understand why you didn't. Bringing me to your home seems a dangerous thing to do. What if I were to escape? Unless you don't plan on letting me live long enough to try."

Those full lips of his pulled into a smile again. "This isna my home. It's…a place to go when needed. More importantly, I doubt ye could even get out of this bed right now, let alone try to escape. Ye lost a great deal of blood." He frowned and straightened the blanket around her.

"But I havena kidnapped ye for any wicked purpose. I simply couldna leave a woman alone on a dangerous country road bleeding her life's blood into the dirt. Especially since I am responsible. I do have some morals. Not many, mind ye," he said with a wink that made her smile despite the situation.

"But a few. When ye are well, ye'll have no need of escape. I'll return ye to yer home. If I was going to kill ye, I wouldna bother healing ye first."

"Oh," she said, relaxing a little. She hadn't thought he'd meant her harm, not when he had taken pains to care for her so thoroughly. But it helped to hear him say it.

"Besides," he continued, "ye were unconscious the entire trip here and ye've yet to see my face. So even if ye *were* to escape, it wouldna do ye much good or me much harm."

He reached over and brushed a lock of hair from her face. She stared into his eyes, wishing she could see the color more clearly, without the shadow from the mask dimming them. She wished she could see more of his face. His hair flowed uncovered to his shoulders. Blond, though not completely. The strands reminded her of the fields of wheat at her grandfather's country estate. Unremarkable until the sun hit them, highlighting the rich golden tones of the stalks.

Most of his face was covered. The mask left only the lower half of his face bare, and what she could see was covered in rough stubble. She had the sudden urge to reach up and run her fingers along his jawline, his full lips. Feel the difference in texture. See if those lips were as soft as they looked. She clenched her hand in a fist and dropped her gaze.

His smug grin left little doubt he knew exactly what path her thoughts had taken. "Yer best chance for a quick recovery is to lie back and get some rest."

She scowled at him but settled back into the pillows. He stared at her, as if there were something else he wanted to say.

A loud sound, like a barn door slamming against a wall, followed by an angry shout made her jump from the bed. Or nearly, in any case. His hand on her good shoulder kept her put. She grunted in pain.

"Rest," he said again. He frowned and glanced out the window before turning back to her. Whatever he'd seen didn't seem to make him happy, but not particularly concerned. "Rest. I promise ye no harm will come to ye under my care."

Her heart pounded in her chest. "You will protect me?"

He regarded her before quietly saying, "I will. Ye have my word."

Again she wished she could see more of his face. The mask did more than hide his features. It hid his emotions as well.

"Why?" she asked. "I am your enemy. Aren't I?"

He smiled at her again. "No, my lady. Ye were never my enemy. And even if ye were, it would make no difference. I'm no' in the habit of harming, or abandoning, defenseless women."

"I'm not defenseless."

His eyes roamed over her bruised and prostrate body, and she grimaced. "Usually, I'm not so defenseless."

His lips twitched. "Aye, I ken that well. Speaking of which…"

He pulled open the drawer of the table near the bed and retrieved her dagger. "I thought ye might like this back. With the agreement," he said, pulling it back from her grasp, "that ye refrain from plunging it into my heart. I am trying to help ye."

Now her lips twitched. "Agreed."

He handed her the dagger, and she slipped it beneath her pillow. Her heart ceased its frantic hammering, and she settled back. Trusting this man was probably the height of folly. Yet, she did.

"What is your name?" she asked.

"Och," he said, breaking into a smile again, "if I told ye that, I'd have to kill ye."

She sighed. "If I'm going to be here awhile, I can't keep calling you the highwayman."

He watched her, then nodded. "Ye can call me Jack."

"Is that your name?"

He hesitated before answering. "Nay. But I'll answer to it."

She frowned, aware the expression bordered on pouting. But she didn't argue with him. Frankly, that he'd given her any name at all surprised her. "All right, then. Jack."

He jerked slightly when the name left her lips. Interesting. It might not be his true name, but she'd be willing to bet her new velvet cloak that it meant something personal to him. A sibling's name maybe? Or a nickname? That would narrow down the possibilities of his real name a bit.

Perhaps the name stood for John? Jackson? Jacob? James? Jason? She'd known men with all those names who preferred to be known as Jack. She'd even had a cousin named Claudius everyone called Jack, so it might come from nothing at all. Perhaps a name he simply pulled from the air. Certainly not something she should be obsessing over, for goodness sake.

"I'll return shortly," he said. After making sure the blankets still snugly covered her, he grabbed the sword that had been propped against a chair near the bed and hurried out of the cottage.

Elizabet sighed and covered her face with her hand. She had no idea how she'd gotten herself into this mess. Or how she'd get out of it. Or what kind of fool she was for trusting a highwayman who'd stolen from her father, gotten her shot, and then kidnapped her in order to heal her. At least she hoped that was the only reason. What kind of highwayman brought his victims back to his hideout to patch them up? Though notorious for his charm and manners, certainly this went above and beyond—even for his tales.

She yawned, sleep pulling at her again. This so-called highwayman baffled her. His speech and mannerisms suggested a gentleman. Not English, certainly, but a gentleman nonetheless. Yet he traveled the roads robbing coaches in the middle of the night. What sort of gentleman did that?

An incredibly well-informed one, for certain. He'd known her father had carried around a ridiculous fortune. Even her mother hadn't known that, judging by the look on her face when the sacks had been pulled from beneath the bench. The robbery had been no circumstance of chance, either. The highwayman and his band had lain in wait for them specifically.

Why?

Too many questions with no answers floated through her head. With slim chance of having them answered.

The rumble of male voices outside the window soon faded into the background as her eyes grew heavy and finally closed. She drifted away to sleep, the vision of blue, soulful eyes filling her thoughts until she knew no more.

Chapter Five

"Are ye mad?" Philip said, kicking at a bale of hay.

"I couldna leave her there," John said. He leaned against the wall of the small barn near the cottage, watching his cousin pace.

"She'll discover who ye are. Ye'll be finished."

"I keep the mask on whenever I'm near her. She hasna seen my face. I deepen my voice a bit. If we were to run into each other at court, she wouldna recognize me. I think." John ran a hand over his face, relishing the slight breeze that blew across his skin.

"I still say you are mad," Philip insisted.

"What would ye have me do?" John asked, his patience wearing thin. "Leave her to bleed into the dust?"

Philip's frown was nearly a pout. He sighed. "Someone would ha' come along, eventually."

John's brow quirked up, and Philip reluctantly smiled. "Fine," Philip said. "But you canna keep her here. And we must leave. We've never stayed here for more than a night or two. Much longer and we'll attract attention. Besides, the meeting is set for the day after next. Our man willna wait if we are late. There are people waiting for these supplies, the coin…"

"I know," he said. "I think…I think I should take her with us."

Philip's jaw nearly hit the ground. "John…"

"I stitched up her arm. She's young and healthy but is far too weak yet. And I dinna like the fever. I canna leave her here to fend for herself."

"Nay, but ye could send the lass on her way. She has her own people at her own home who can care for her."

"Aye, and if I thought they'd actually do so, I might consider it. But ye know her father. The man is a greedy, selfish bastard who'd sooner hasten her death along than do what he could to heal her. She's unmarried with no children. If she dies, her father will inherit the estates her grandparents left her. Do ye really believe he'd no' welcome that? And now with Fergus in his pocket…" John had to stop and contain the rage roiling inside. "Him being at Barrington Manor last night was no coincidence. I'm more certain than ever they are working together. Why else would Dawsey wed his daughter to a landless, titleless bastard, if not to control her dowry lands through her husband? The daft wee shite doesna even realize Dawsey's made a puppet of him."

"Been thinking on this, have ye?"

"Aye. And I'll no' leave her to their mercy."

Philip sighed. "Glenlyon is a week's journey."

"Not much farther than her own home. And she'll receive much better care at Glenlyon."

"Aye. And then she can go straight to the King's Guard and not only identify you but lead them right to the door of our kin. Is that what ye want?"

"O' course not. And I wouldna take her to the keep. Perhaps to one of the cottages. There are a few secluded ones where no one will disturb us, and she can heal while being none the wiser as to where she is."

"Oh? And what of you? Will ye keep that mask on the whole time?"

John frowned but nodded. Philip snorted. "That'll be comfortable."

John ignored that. "Where's Will?"

Philip grinned. "Dinna worry about him. I've set him to enough chores it'll be months before he has any energy or desire to go on a job again. And I'm holding onto his pistol until he's a little less heavy on the trigger."

"Good thinking."

"I dinna like this plan, John. It's dangerous. For her and us."

"I ken that well. But I'll no' leave her behind."

"Then we should leave immediately. Traveling with the lass as she is will take longer. We canna miss our contact."

"Agreed. And I dinna want to take the risk of her worsening."

Philip slapped his hat against his leg and shook his head with a sigh. "You take the lass on to Glenlyon. I'll take the load on to our man."

"I canna let ye do that alone."

"I'll take Will."

John's eyes widened. "I think ye'd be better off alone."

Philip laughed. "He's no' so bad. A might eager, perhaps. A nice long journey with lots of hard labor will calm him a bit. We'll manage fine."

"Philip…"

"Go. I can deliver a wagonload of supplies without ye. I'm not totally helpless, ye ken."

"Aye, I know," he said, clapping his kinsman on the shoulder.

Philip looked at him, concern etched on his face. "I hope

ye ken what ye're doing."

John gave him a wry smile. "Not an ounce. But I'll tread carefully."

"I hope so. She is the daughter of Lord Dawsey, after all."

John's smile changed to a scowl. "She's nothing like him."

"Are ye willing to bet yer life on that?"

"Yes," John said quietly.

They'd spent only an hour together. Not enough time to know for certain that he could place his faith in her. But the woman had strength, kindness, intelligence, and bravery. And a beauty so brilliant it set his chest to aching. Could he trust her? Maybe not. He would take the necessary precautions to protect those who depended on him.

But he couldn't leave her. Not newly stitched and burning with a fever due to his mistake. Not when anything might happen to her. The urge to shelter and care for her overwhelmed him with an intensity too strong to ignore. The image of his mother, burning with fever in childbed, came to his mind, and he immediately forced it away.

He wouldn't let that happen to Elizabet, no matter what risks he had to take. The fault for her injuries lay at his feet. His man had shot her. The responsibility for her now fell to him, and he'd do everything in his power to ensure she made it home, whole and healthy.

Hopefully, he wouldn't regret it.

He looked up to find Philip staring at him, either in concern or bemusement, John couldn't tell. John straightened away from the wall.

"Dinna worry. You keep an eye on Will. We'll meet at the ruins three weeks from tonight. Then perhaps we'll discover what Dawsey and that fiend Fergus have been up to."

Philip mounted his horse and nodded. "Take care."

John smiled and slapped the horse's rump. His smile faded, though, as his kinsman rode out of sight. Philip had cause to be worried. Elizabet's presence at his hideaway presented a danger to him. And his men. Bringing her to his home would only bring danger to more people he loved, if he didn't have a care.

Of course, he wanted her gone as soon as possible.

He kept repeating that to himself as he walked back to the cottage. Maybe by the time he entered and came face-to-face with her he'd believe it.

· · ·

They rocked and swayed over the pitted trail, but Jack had padded the wagon bed so well she hardly felt a bump. Which was a blessing because her arm ached and burned until her teeth were on edge. She shivered and huddled beneath the blankets. How she could be cold when her face nearly pulsed with heat, she didn't know. The answer should be easy enough. But her mind seemed to be floating in a hazy fog.

They'd been traveling for several days, stopping only for brief rests. They'd avoided inns and other people in general, sleeping in the wagon for a few hours at night with Jack sitting close enough to share his warmth, but not so close as to jostle her arm. The days blurred into one another. He offered her food whenever they stopped. Travel rations from his saddlebag. He never once left her to hunt. She found it sweet, really. As sweet as a captor taking care of his captive could be.

The thought uppermost in her mind should have been escape. Or at least her own health. She had enough lucid periods to know she wasn't doing well but in those rare clear moments, she thought only of getting a glimpse of Jack's face. She probably should have been more concerned with where he was taking her. All he would say was someplace safe. He worried about her. Quite considerate of him, bearing in mind her injuries had been caused during the robbery of her family. But still, even with all those pressing issues, she couldn't stop wondering what he looked like.

He couldn't wear his mask, of course. Not while they traveled in broad daylight. They kept off the main roads, and Jack seemed to have a knack for avoiding other people because as far as she knew, they hadn't seen anyone. Even still, he kept on a low-brimmed hat pulled over his brow to shadow his face, with a scarf against the chill in the air that covered everything but his eyes. Seemed like she should be able to piece together the bottom half of his face from when he wore the mask, with the top half of his face, shadowed though it was. Only she couldn't make her mind work like that. She couldn't make it work at all.

The wagon rumbled over a particularly bumpy patch of road, and she moaned before she could stop herself.

They pulled to a halt, and Jack's face appeared above her. All covered or shadowed. She wanted to see his eyes, but his hand came down to gently feel her forehead, effectively blocking her vision at the same time.

"Ye have a fever still." A cool cloth touched her forehead, and she leaned in to it gratefully, even as her body racked with shivers. He helped her sit up enough to drink some water from his skin.

"Where?" she managed to say.

"We're almost there. Another few hours." He laid her back down. Before she could glance up, his hand covered her eyes again, and he stroked her face, from her forehead to her chin as her mother used to do when she was a child.

"Rest, lass. We'll be there soon."

She fought to stay awake, but the fever pulled her under.

• • •

When she finally swam up from under the fog, she found herself out of the wagon and tucked into a warm, comfortable bed. She glanced around but recognized nothing. They must have finally arrived at Jack's hideout. Speaking of Jack…

"Hello there," he said, quietly closing the door behind him. To her disappointment he had his mask on once again.

"Where are we?" she asked, for lack of anything better to say. And she really wanted to know.

"In a small cottage, near my home."

"Scotland?"

"Aye."

"I've never been to Scotland."

Jack smiled and wrapped an arm about her to help her sit. He handed her a cup that smelled of herbs and honey.

"Once ye're feeling better, I'll take ye outside and show ye what ye've been missing."

"I do actually feel much better. I must have needed some rest." She took a sip of the tea, looking up when Jack laughed. "What?"

"Ye needed the rest, all right. Ye've been asleep for nigh on three days now."

"What?" She sat forward so quickly the tea sloshed over the edge of the cup, and Jack hurriedly took it from her. While shocked at how long she'd been unconscious, sitting without her arm throbbing in pain pleased her. At least she'd been spared a few days of uncomfortable healing.

"Old Granny Mc…Granny Mac has been caring for ye. Ye had a raging fever when we first arrived. I wasna sure what to do for ye. It's why I brought ye here in the first place. I knew Granny could fix ye right up. Here," he said, handing her back the tea. "Drink this up. Granny's had me pouring that down yer throat since we arrived. And seeing as how fit yer feeling, I'd say it's working."

Elizabet nodded, agreeing.

Jack jumped up at the sound of a wagon outside. After a quick peek out the window, he cursed quietly beneath his breath and went to open the door.

"What are ye doing here?" he asked.

"Well, and that's a fine hello," a feminine voice said from the doorway.

"Hello, Cousin." The affectionate smile evident in his voice piqued her curiosity about the woman. A kinswoman of Jack's would be a wealth of information. Hopefully. She didn't sound like a kinswoman. Though she had a faint Scottish brogue, her underlying speech was thoroughly English.

"Are you going to explain the mask?" she asked.

"No."

Well that answered one question. He apparently didn't wear it all the time. Elizabet had begun to wonder.

"Are you going to explain why you've been here half a week and haven't been to say hello?"

"Ah…no."

"Well, then. Are you going to invite me in or leave me standing in your yard?"

Elizabet smiled. She liked this woman already.

"How did ye know I was up here?"

A delicate snort sounded. "The whole valley knew of your return three days before you did."

Jack chuckled. "Aye. Word does travel quickly in the Highlands."

"That's an understatement." The woman stepped inside and hugged Jack, though her back was still to Elizabet. "It's good to see you, J—"

"Jack."

There was a slight pause and Elizabet wished she could see the woman's face.

"Jack," she repeated, her tone full of question. And amusement. "Well now, let's see if the rest of the rumors are true…"

She turned and saw Elizabet sitting propped up in the bed. "I see the gossipmongers haven't disappointed us this time." She glanced back at Jack. "I asked you to bring me back a present from England J…Jack. But this isn't quite what I had in mind."

"She is far prettier than anything else I saw there," he said, smiling and looking straight at Elizabet, who couldn't help the blush that crept to her cheeks.

"Indeed," the woman said, turning an amused and speculative grin on him.

Jack pulled her to the side and spoke low enough Elizabet couldn't hear. Though, from the woman's expression, which alternated between surprised, dismayed, and worried, Elizabet assumed he explained their predicament. She finally nodded and patted his arm before making her way over.

Elizabet watched her as she came toward the bed. With her raven hair and striking blue eyes, the woman's beauty made Elizabet look drab in comparison. She gave Elizabet a warm smile and sat beside her on the bed.

"And how are you feeling this morning?" she asked, leaning forward to feel Elizabet's head. "The fever appears to have broken."

"I'm quite well. A bit sore," she said, nodding at her arm. "But well otherwise. Thank you."

"Very glad to hear it. Granny sent me over to check on you. Poor dear is feeling a bit under the weather herself." She fussed over her a bit longer, making sure all was well. "Another few days I think and you'll be right as rain, Miss…?"

"Elizabet. Harding," she said.

The woman's gaze flicked briefly to Jack. "I'm very pleased to meet you, Lady Elizabet."

Elizabet frowned. "You know of my father, then?"

"I've heard mention of him a time or two," she said, her

gaze straying back to Jack before returning to Elizabet. "And you must call me—"

"Don't tell her who ye are," Jack said.

The woman rolled her eyes. "My name is Sorcha MacGregor," she said.

Jack blew out a breath, threw his hands up, and went to pace in front of the hearth.

"Sorcha?" Elizabet said, her eyes widening in recognition. "I remember you. Or, I've heard of you, at least. At court. Your hasty wedding was quite the gossip for a time."

Sorcha's delicate black brows rose. "Was it now?"

"Oh, yes. Everyone chattered about how you'd been forced to marry the great Scottish beast they called the Lion, dragged up here and no one ever heard from you again."

Sorcha laughed. "Well, he can be a bit beastly when the mood strikes him, but he's not so bad."

Elizabet gave her a smile. "Happy to hear it, my lady."

Seeing Sorcha so happy did truly ease Elizabet's troubled heart some. She'd thought of the gossip surrounding Sorcha often, ever since her father had entered into negotiations with Fergus. A poor English girl being forced to marry a Scottish brute? Their fates had seemed parallel. Though somehow, Elizabet didn't think she'd have such a happy ending as Sorcha, if she married Fergus. He didn't seem the type to care about the happiness of his bride.

Sorcha must have been thinking along the same lines. "I have a feeling your wedding may surpass mine with the gossip, particularly after this adventure."

Elizabet nodded, then frowned. "If there is a wedding. Who would marry a woman who's gone missing for several weeks, especially if it is known with whom I'm missing?"

"Yes," Sorcha said, flashing a raised eyebrow back at Jack. "Though perhaps that is for the best. I can't imagine any marriage that includes my half brother having a happy ending."

Elizabet's gaze flew to Sorcha, her body nearly trembling with shock. "Your half brother?"

Sorcha nodded. "Fergus Campbell. Or...whatever he is calling himself these days. We share a father. And very little else. While I'd welcome a beautiful new sister," she said with a soft smile, "I wouldn't wish Fergus on anyone. Perhaps Jack has done you more of a favor than he intended."

Elizabet glanced over to where Jack leaned against the wall, watching them while keeping an eye on the courtyard through the window.

"Perhaps he has," she agreed. He looked over, and their gazes met. The smile he gave her sent a fine tremble through her body, and she bit her bottom lip, hoping the small, sharp pain would refocus her mind on Sorcha instead of the devilishly handsome rogue who gazed at her with such intensity.

Before she could say anything else, the door opened again and an older woman carrying an overflowing basket and an armful of clothing bustled in. She deposited everything on the table and looked around with disapproval, her frown deepening when she caught sight of Elizabet in the bed.

"Really. What is it with you MacGregors? The lot of you can't be trusted at all. At least not with respectable English ladies." She glanced at him, barely changing expression when she saw the mask. "Can't say I'm surprised," she said, flicking a finger at it.

"Ah, Berta!" Jack said, sweeping the old woman into his arms and twirling her about. "Ye know we canna resist you beautiful English roses."

He gave her a sound kiss and set a now giggling Berta back on her feet.

"Oh, you," she said, giving him a playful push.

Elizabet couldn't help smiling at his charming antics.

She should probably be screaming, begging these women for help. But Jack had done nothing to threaten her. He hadn't even been the one to injure her in the first place and had gone to great lengths to bring her back to health.

Being so far from home *did* concern her somewhat. Then again, for the first time in her life, her parents couldn't touch her. Couldn't force an unwanted marriage to a loathsome man on her. Eventually, she would have to return. But until then, she would relish her small taste of freedom and enjoy the adventure of it all. And if that meant spending a little more time with a charming highwayman, that was a sacrifice she would willingly make.

Chapter Six

Elizabet stretched her arm. Though still tender and bruised, it was well on its way to healing. There was no reason she couldn't travel. Yet still, Jack made no mention of taking her home. Far from finding this disturbing, the opportunity to extend her stay thrilled Elizabet. She didn't remember her first several days at Glenlyon, of course. But since she'd woken a few days before, she'd been thoroughly enjoying her time at the cottage. Jack kept her warm, comfortable, and she had a breathtaking view of the loch from the window by the bed. She'd been visited twice more by the lovely Sorcha, whose charm, beauty, and confidence made her someone Elizabet would very much enjoy getting to know better. And every other waking minute had been spent with the man she should probably loathe.

Speaking of...

The door to the small cottage opened, and Jack came in, carrying a stack of wood.

"Ah, ye're awake. How are ye feeling today?"

"Better, thank you." She watched him as he set the wood

down by the fire, admiring the bunching of his muscles. The way his shirt pulled taut across his back. The glimpses of his calves and knees when his plaid moved. She'd never considered knees to be particularly attractive before. Until she'd seen his.

He turned and caught her gaze. She looked quickly away but not before she saw his amused smile.

He came to sit by her. "I hope ye're comfortable."

"I am, thank you."

"I'm sure this is a far cry from yer family's estates. Or the palace's marbled halls, if ye stay at the court of our illustrious king."

Elizabet cocked her head, considering him. "You don't seem to like our king overly much."

"Och, I like him fine enough. It's his policies I dinna always approve of, or his reluctance to enforce some of them, I should say."

"Seems as though you benefit from some of those lax laws," she said with a small smile.

He gave her an answering smile. "I may break a few laws from time to time in order to right a few others."

Before she could respond, he stood and looked around the cottage. "I didna mean to disturb yer rest, but I wanted to see if there was anything ye needed…"

"I'm fine, thank you. You may find it strange, but I haven't missed the comforts of home all that much. In fact, it's been a relief to get away from the relentless pressure to always behave a certain way. After all, a slovenly, unattractive girl will never catch herself a wealthy husband. According to my mother, at least, that is my sole purpose in life. Therefore, most of her waking moments are put to obtaining the best match possible."

"Well, I could nag ye a bit more, if it would make ye feel more at home. Or bring Berta by. The woman could nag the devil himself into being a saint."

That surprised a laughing snort out of her. She slapped a hand over her mouth, mortified. But far from being appalled, Jack laughed. A great, loud belly laugh that made Elizabet laugh along with him.

This is what she loved. With Jack, she could be herself. The man was insanely difficult to coax into speech. At least anything of a personal nature. But he accepted her without question. A refreshing change that she relished.

"Let's see to yer arm now, shall we?" he asked, gently unwrapping her bandage.

She'd come to look forward to the hour when he'd re-dress her shoulder. She'd never known anyone so large to be so gentle. From the way his fingers skimmed across her skin to how he carefully wrapped the linen around her arm. Each brush of his hand sent a riot of sensations rushing through her body. She swore he lingered far longer than necessary. He must be as affected as she. She'd been well enough to travel for a couple of days, and she did worry about her parents. Surely even they were concerned for her. But she would be going home soon enough. For now, she tried to put everything else from her mind so she could savor these moments of freedom.

"What are ye thinking about so fiercely?" he asked, reaching for a new bandage.

She shrugged with her uninjured shoulder. "Only that you seem perfectly happy to listen to me chatter away about whatever nonsense enters my head, but you don't reciprocate much."

"Do ye expect me to?"

"No, not really. After all, you still wear that ridiculous mask when you are near me. Naturally, I can't expect you to be going about spilling all your secrets."

"But?"

She smiled. "I suppose I find it odd that I feel so

comfortable saying anything at all to you when truthfully, I don't know you at all. And under the circumstances..."

"I'm not who ye'd expect as a confidant, eh?"

"Something like that."

"So what sorts of things can ye tell me that would scandalize less disreputable folk?"

She shook her head. "Nothing in particular comes to mind."

"Och, come now. What is the last thing yer mother scolded ye for?"

Elizabet laughed. "What hasn't she scolded me for might be easier to tell you."

A blond eyebrow rose over the mask, and she sighed. "Well, the last thing I said that truly horrified her, other than my wish to avoid the match with Mr. Ramsay, of course, was that church services bore me to tears."

Jack gasped and sat back from her. "Heathen!"

Elizabet giggled. "And that I thought the king's mistress, the Countess of Castlemaine, is actually quite lovely and entertaining company. Personally, I applaud her. She is wealthy, powerful, and she and the king seem quite happy together—when he isn't with his wife or another mistress. Still, she has the run of court, acts in any way she pleases, and has the king himself showering her with whatever she wishes. There are worse ways to live."

"Aye, that's true enough."

"Had I said those things to my mother, I'd have been slapped and sent to my room without supper. At best. My mother plays nice when at court but does nothing but spew judgment and condemnation in private."

"Oh, aye. I prefer to spew my judgment and condemnation openly. Hence, the mask and odd nightly activities."

"Well, I don't know how open it is, if you're hiding behind that mask," she said, resisting the urge to reach out and pluck it off.

But again, Jack merely smiled. "There's being open and being daft. I'll tell those I judge why I condemn them. But I dinna see the benefit in letting them know more about me than they already do."

"They might disagree."

"I'm certain they do. Then again, I'm no' asking their opinion on the matter." He winked at her and finished binding her arm before tucking her blanket firmly about her.

She'd worn nothing but a chemise around him in the days she'd been there. Jack had said her gown was in the armoire. But it would be too uncomfortable and out of place in her current surroundings. And as she mostly stayed in bed or sat in a chair by the window, she'd seen no need to do more than wrap a quilt about her for modesty. Though he'd already seen more than the quilt would cover anyway. Another fact that would horrify her mother.

"Yer arm is almost good as new." He stood and cleaned up his bandage supplies. "Is there aught ye need?"

"I've been cooped up in here for days now. Can't I go outside for a bit?"

He finished putting the strips of linen and ointment away before he answered. "I suppose I could allow that. For a short time," he warned.

She nodded eagerly, and he watched her, as if he were trying to gauge the safety of allowing her more freedom.

"Would it help if I promised not to run off?" she said.

He grinned at that. "Wouldna matter if ye did. Ye wouldna get far. All right, then." He pulled back the blanket and helped her up, slipping a pair of boots onto her feet that Sorcha had brought for her.

He wrapped a thick shawl about her shoulders and led her outside. Elizabet took a deep breath of the crisp, fresh air and smiled, turning her face up to the sun. The cottage sat nestled in a small clearing on a wooded hill. A brook babbled nearby, but she heard no voices or sounds that would indicate other people were in the area.

Jack took her hand and led her up a small trail, matching his pace to hers. When they came out of the trees, Elizabet looked around, her breath catching in a quiet gasp. From atop their hill, she could see the whole valley below them. A modest castle stood proud and majestic on the banks of a loch, a small village spread out around it. The sun shone off the water, glistening against the gentle loll of the waves.

"It's so beautiful," she said, in awe of her surroundings.

"Aye, that it is."

"This is your home?"

He nodded. "I grew up here, though I have my own lands. Just over that ridge," he said, pointing to a row of hills in the distance. "But there's nothing there but a pile of rubble that used to be my home."

"What happened to it?"

"The keep and surrounding fields were destroyed in the skirmishes with the Campbells. My father wanted to rebuild. But he died before he could."

"Will you rebuild?"

He shrugged. "I suppose I might. Someday. But I always have a home here, if I need one."

She glanced up at him. "Why do you leave here to roam the roads to London? Weren't you happy?"

He gave her a faint smile, though his gaze stayed on the scene below. "Some things are more important than my own happiness."

He took a deep breath and seemed to shake off his seriousness as a dog would divest itself of water. "Come. There's a small brook not far from here with a great clump of berry bushes."

"Berries? It seems ages since I had fresh berries."

"Well, then. We shall gorge ourselves until we can hold no more."

She took his hand eagerly and made to follow, except in her haste she let part of her shawl trail on the ground. The fabric wound about her ankle, entangling her already unsteady feet. She didn't have a chance.

Jack attempted to stop her headlong plunge down the slope of the hill. Instead, she managed to pull him with her. He did at least slow her enough that she didn't topple end over end all the way to the bottom. But they left a nice trail of disturbed earth in their path as they careened down.

As soon as they stopped tumbling, Jack immediately crawled over to her. "Are ye all right, lass?"

She grunted in reply, and he gave her an amused grin, though concern still creased his brow. He ran his hands over her, checking her ribs, her limbs, and gently probed her shoulder. She sucked in a breath at that.

"How is it?" he asked.

"I'll do," she said, though she briefly considered curling into a ball and moaning until the throbbing went away.

"Can ye sit?"

She narrowed her eyes. "Probably. I hadn't planned on it, though."

He laughed and wrapped an arm around her to help her up. "Come on, then. It would be best if we didna sit down here all the day long."

"Really? Sounds like a fine idea to me."

"Och. Yer're stronger than that." He stood and pulled her up and into his arms. "But I'd be happy to assist ye all the same."

She should resist. Tell him to put her down. But she had no intention of doing either of those things, because being in his arms fulfilled her dearest desire. So she wrapped an arm about his neck and let him hold her.

The time drew near when she'd have to leave. She probably should have already returned home. She didn't ask about it, though. She was dangerously close to wanting to stay forever.

Until then, she would embrace being rash and irresponsible.

. . .

John gathered Elizabet closer and began the trek back up the hill. Her warmth mingled with his, the light floral smell that was uniquely hers enveloped him. She could have walked on her own, but he'd not give up the opportunity to have her in his arms. No matter how ill-advised.

He carried her to the brook, then set her gently down, kneeling beside her.

"Are ye sure ye're no' injured," he said, his eyes roving over her for any sign of blood or damage.

"I promise, I am well. A little bruised, perhaps. But I'll do."

He reached out and pulled a few twigs from her hair, looking at them with a soft grin. "I wouldna think lesser of ye if ye were hurt, ye ken?"

She returned his smile. "I know. But I truly am fine. My pride, on the other hand, has taken quite a blow."

John chuckled lightly. "When I was a lad, my brother fell down a hill, though not so steep as the one with which ye just became acquainted. He screeched and blethered until our mother threatened to beat him soundly and give him something to go on about. You made hardly a sound and shed not one tear. Your pride is safe, lass."

He hadn't moved his hand, but instead continued to lightly stroke her hair. Far from finding this insulting, she leaned into his touch. He cupped her cheek, and her eyes nearly fluttered closed.

This bordered on madness. She was the daughter of his enemy. And for all rights and purposes, his hostage. He should be ransoming her back to her father. Yet all he could think of were those big brown eyes of hers dancing with laughter. Her soft skin beneath his touch. The velvety softness of her lips under his thumb. He'd watched his cousin find happiness with Sorcha and, while he'd envied them to a point, it had never been something he especially desired. The life of domestic bliss was not for him. He craved excitement, adventure. He never thought he'd want anything more.

Until her. Elizabet sparked a craving in him for an excitement and adventure of a different sort. If he could find happiness with one person in the world, chances were good she was the one. That the possibility didn't exist meant he should shove the idea from his mind as fast as he could. But he didn't want to let go yet. "I believe I promised ye some berries," he said.

"I believe you did." She smiled up at him, and his heart must have knocked into a lung, because he suddenly found it difficult to pull in a full breath. Her beauty at that moment, with her hair in a tangle and dirt smudging her face, would make even the angels in heaven cry.

He led her to the clump of bushes that grew in the shelter of the woods, grinning at her delighted gasp.

"Bilberries!" she said, reaching out to pluck one. She popped it in her mouth, her eyes closing as she chewed.

"We call them blaeberries. Shall we take some back with us?"

"Please. Oh, but we didn't bring a basket."

"Nay worries. We can carry them in my kilt."

He reached down to lift the front of his kilt, and she rewarded him with a scandalized shriek before slapping the fabric out of his hand. He grinned. "Ye didna wish for any berries, then?"

"I'll carry them." She gathered a few folds of her skirts to form a pocket.

"But, lass." He leaned closer as if to impart a secret. "Ye're exposing a bit of flesh if ye do that." He nodded down at the inch of ankle now visible.

She raised a brow. "A far sight better than what you'd be exposing," she said.

His laugh echoed through the woods.

They gathered enough berries to fill her skirt and then sat on the banks of the creek to eat their fill.

"Oh," she said, glancing down at a tear in her skirt. "I must have caught it on a branch."

He examined the rend. "Och, it's no' but a small tear. I can mend it for ye."

Her eyes widened. "You do your own mending?"

"Of course. Most men spend a fair amount of time away from home, hunting or fighting. We'd all be running about naked as the day we're born if we couldna throw a stitch or two. I could knit ye a nice pair of stockings if ye have need as well," he said with a wink.

She squinted at him. "I don't believe you."

"No?"

He rummaged in his sporran, coming out with a needle shoved in a bit of cork, already threaded. Then he gathered her skirt, his hand tightening on the material with the sudden urge to delve beneath it. She watched him, her breath catching in her throat. He tugged on the skirt so she had to scoot closer. The temptation burned through him. So strong. She must have known it. Felt it. Yet, she did nothing but move even closer to him, until her skirts pooled in his lap and her bare legs were inches from his own.

He swallowed hard and dragged in a slow breath, trying to calm the buzzing in his head and the fire in his blood. The lass was still healing. And even if she were not, he'd not take her like some rutting animal on the dirty banks of a creek. Not the first time. And not under these circumstances. Even if she was willing.

He relaxed his hold on her skirts and spread the material out so he could properly line up the torn fabric. The tension between them eased as he made quick work of the tear, both of them focused on the mundane task rather than their proximity to each other.

When he finished, she examined her skirt with delight. "It looks good as new."

"Well, almost," he said, though a warm pleasure at her praise spread through him.

"I'm impressed."

He waved that off. "Och, it's nothing but a task even the wee ones can do. I've been mending most of my own clothes since I was a lad."

She laughed. "I'm trying to picture my father sitting before the fire knitting his own stockings. I don't think he's ever pulled his own stockings on, let alone mended them."

The mention of her father sobered John, bringing him back to an unwelcome reality where, by all rights, the woman before him should be firmly in the enemy camp. He couldn't see her as such, though. No matter how he tried. She wasn't his enemy. She was…Elizabet.

He reached out and wiped the small smudge of dark-red juice from her lip, and she froze. But she didn't pull away. Instead, her lips parted with a small sigh. The heat from her mouth warmed his thumb, beckoned to him. He leaned forward, pressing his lips to hers in a kiss so gentle he could have imagined it.

She pulled back enough to meet his gaze, though she stayed within the circle of his arms. "You said you wouldn't kiss me until I asked," she said with a small smile.

"Ye can ask me later."

He cupped her face and brought her closer, tasting the sweet juice on her lips. She melted with a soft moan, and he crushed her to him, his blood roaring in his veins.

His lips moved over hers, urging them to part. He delved inside, drawing her closer when another moan escaped her. He needed to stop. Now. Before the mad desire raging through his body at her touch completely consumed them both. And then she draped tentative arms around his neck. Her fingers tangled in his hair, drawing him deeper. And he was lost. Let the consequences happen as they would. Every last one of them would be well worth it, if he could spend five more minutes in her arms.

The sound of leaves crunching was his only warning that someone had discovered them.

He jumped up and spun around, his dagger in his hand, already crouched in a battle stance.

Malcolm looked at him, eyebrows raised. John gave his cousin a sheepish smile.

"I'm surprised ye let me get so close," Malcolm said, a gentle rebuke in his voice. John sheathed his dagger with a frown. Malcolm was right. Had he been an enemy, it might have been too late. And Elizabet would have been in danger.

"It won't happen again," he promised. He turned around to help Elizabet to her feet. "Lady Elizabet, may I present Malcolm MacGregor, Laird of Glenlyon."

Her eyes shot to John's, no doubt in surprise that he'd introduce her to someone so prominent. Though with Sorcha visiting frequently and making no secret of her identity, Elizabet already knew their location. It mattered little now if she met everyone at the keep. Then again, the more people she met, the more likely she could discover his identity. He wasn't sure he cared anymore, though he should.

She gave Malcolm a quick little curtsy, and he nodded at

her. "My wife has brought ye some stew and bread, I believe, as well as fresh clothing." His eyes briefly traveled over the stained chemise visible beneath her shawl. Though merely cursory, blandly curious at most, John had the sudden urge to protect Elizabet from the other man's gaze. He stepped in front of her, and Malcolm's eyes widened. John hadn't realized he'd moved until Malcolm gave him that look. And the amused shake of his head did nothing to improve John's mood.

Elizabet moved out from behind him and watched their visitor with curious eyes. He didn't like that she wouldn't stay put and let him protect her. But the fact that she put him at her back, all her focus on Malcolm, spoke of a trust in John that sent a thrill through him he'd never felt before. One that he had no right to feel. Still, he reveled in the fact that she trusted him to guard her back instead of feeling the need to protect herself from him.

"Go on up the path there," he said, pointing it out to her. "The cottage is right at the top. Shout if ye need me."

"I can see why they call you the Lion," she said to Malcolm, completely ignoring John's request. He took a deep breath. She may trust him, but that apparently didn't extend to following his orders.

Malcolm gave her a wry smile. "Aye?"

"The hair, the eyes…"

"Elizabet," John said.

Her gaze switched to him, and he jerked his head toward the trail. She opened her mouth to protest again, and he gave her the sternest look he could muster, though part of him wanted to laugh at her temerity. In a strange place, faced with a man like Malcolm, and her natural inclination was to interrogate him.

She sighed and flounced away. As soon as she was safely out of sight, John took his mask off and rubbed his face.

"Do ye never take it off in front of her?" Malcolm asked.

"No. Was there something ye needed, Cousin?"

Malcolm's damnable eyebrow rose again. "Aye. I need my able-minded kinsman back. He seems to have been replaced with a madman who doesna ken his arse from his head."

John looked at Malcolm with surprise and then shook his head with an amused smile. "As bad as all that, is it?"

"Worse."

"Aye, I ken. But there doesna seem to be a damn thing I can do about it."

Malcolm shook his head and chuckled. "They do have a way of mixing a man up, no doubt about it. But ye need to stop this, John. Ye're putting more than yer own life at risk."

John sighed and ran his hand through his hair. "That wasna my intention, Cousin."

"Aye, but that's no matter now. Is she betrothed to that bastard Fergus Campbell?"

John scowled, trying to tamp down the sudden burst of fury that flowed through him at that name. "Not officially, I dinna believe."

"Well, according to the messenger who arrived today, he apparently believes otherwise and is being a nuisance at court, though so far only among certain circles. Her parents are apparently trying to keep the whole situation quiet. But Fergus has been petitioning the king and trying to rally discreet support to find her and to capture the Highland Highwayman so that he might be brought to justice for the heinous crime he's committed in taking her. He won't stay discreet for long."

John shook his head. "He wants her family connections and her estates. I have my suspicions as to why, but no proof as yet. He doesna love her."

Malcolm's eyes widened at that. "Do you?"

John's gaze shot up. "Of course not. I've only just met

the lass."

"Aye, well, sometimes that's all it takes. I knew the moment my own new bride held a dagger to my throat on our wedding night that she was my true mate. And we'd known each other only a day. Though we were both stubborn about it. Once we truly got to know each other…well, if it's the same for you…"

John had a sudden image of Elizabet pulling a dagger on him as well. What was it about a woman wielding a blade that made her so irresistible?

He sighed. "No. It's not."

Truthfully, he didn't know what he felt for her. He wanted to protect her, make her laugh, spend hours talking to her, spend hours doing nothing but being with her. And spend hours kissing her until she moaned his name and begged him to take her. But love? It couldn't be that. They'd known each other only a couple weeks. He wasn't even sure what love was. And even if he did, he could never act on it.

The last thing he wanted was a woman in his life. Women were fragile, even the strong ones. Too much could happen he couldn't protect them from. Especially a headstrong woman like Elizabet. Oh, he loved the fire in her. But it made her reckless. He'd never felt so out of control with a woman in his life, and it unsettled him far more than he cared to admit. He'd lost too many women he loved to ever allow himself to love another. His mother in childbed. His sister to a fever. But he couldn't deny Elizabet had ignited something within him.

The time had definitely come for him to return her home. "No," he said again, though even he could tell his heart wasn't in it.

"Are ye sure, John?" Malcolm asked quietly. He'd known John since they were boys. Had been raised together like brothers. No one knew him better. Most of the time John cherished that connection. Now was not one of those times.

"What I feel for the lass doesna matter. She is better off far away from me. But I dinna like abandoning her to that bastard Campbell."

"Neither do I. We'll find out what he is up to. For all our sakes. I doubt he's forgotten our part in his downfall."

"Aye, that's the honest truth."

"Regardless, the lass needs to go back. It's one thing if ye mean to offer for her. But she's no' a pet, John. Ye canna keep her."

"I ken that well enough," he snapped. Then he sighed. "Apologies, Malcolm. Ye dinna need to tell me. I'll take her home. We'll leave tomorrow."

"Ye needn't rush off quite so soon. Ye can take a few days—"

"No. It's time."

Malcolm watched him, and John tried not to squirm under his gaze. "All right, then. I'll send Tim up with supplies for your journey." He clasped John's shoulder. "Be safe, Cousin. And return soon."

"I will," John said, his heart heavy. He'd return when he could, and his life would go back to what it had been. And it would be lonelier and sadder for what he'd almost known and lost. But there was no help for that. They were no good for each other. Though if any a woman came close, it was her.

He watched Malcolm walk away, and then he donned his mask and turned back to his cottage where Elizabet waited.

Chapter Seven

Elizabet patted the horse, giving his nose a good rub. "Must we continue on so soon? Surely resting for a day or two wouldn't do any harm."

Jack gave her a small, intimate smile, the type she'd only dreamed of getting from a man. While she didn't look forward to returning home and all that it entailed, the actual journey had been far more pleasurable than spending all day on a horse should be. Largely due to the fact that she had to ride with Jack, nestled in the cocoon of his arms. Several days of such riding had made her strangely attuned to him.

He boosted her onto the horse and settled in behind her. "Dinna fash. We should arrive at the cottage in a few hours. Then tomorrow, I'll take ye to a place where ye can arrange to be taken home."

Her heart fell. "So soon? I thought it would take longer."

His only response was to tighten his arms about her and nudge the horse onward. In truth, they'd been traveling for nearly a week, sleeping in the rough in the wee hours of the night and traveling as many hours as they could sit the horse.

She'd spent every instant completely wrapped up in Jack. Her senses filled with the masculine scent of him, her body becoming accustomed to every shift of his muscles, every beat of his heart. He held her so gently, yet firmly enough to keep her secure. She would have been happy had the journey taken a month, despite the discomforts of travel.

The secret of his true identity still ate at her. He was a MacGregor almost certainly. And someone who commanded respect. Someone close to the laird of Glenlyon and his family. Perhaps Jack was family as well. Not that his family mattered so much to her. But she longed to know his true name.

She turned her face in to his chest, nuzzling against him. He murmured something to her. Gaelic words that she couldn't understand, though she could guess, as his arms tightened about her again and his lips grazed her neck. She tilted her head, giving him better access. If she only had a few more hours with him, she had every intention of making the most of them. She raised her arm, reaching behind her to thread her fingers through the hair at the nape of his neck. Keeping his lips imprisoned on her skin. His tongue darted out, tasting her, and she gasped and arched against him. He whispered again, more unintelligible words that still branded themselves on her heart.

When his teeth gently nipped at her neck, she twisted around, fusing her lips to his. The movements of the horse beneath them created a rocking motion that had her nearly dizzy with desire and craving his touch. She turned as far as she could, trying to get closer. Her body ached for something she didn't know how to ask for. All she knew was that she wanted more. Wanted his hands on her skin. His lips on her body. *Him*. All of him.

He kissed down the column of her throat, his lips trailing over every inch of exposed skin he could reach until he finally stopped, wrenching himself from her with a great intake of breath.

"Enough, lass. I canna bear to touch so much of you and yet so little."

"Then touch more," she said, the heat beating through her giving her a confidence she never knew existed.

He rested his forehead against her temple and drew in another tremulous breath. "I would love nothing more. But doing so would be unforgivable."

She tried to protest further, but he shook his head. "Nay, *leannan*." He kissed her forehead, then drew her head back to his chest. "Rest awhile now. Just let me hold ye."

She took a deep breath and slowly released it, trying to calm the furious beating of her heart. She knew he was right. In a few short hours, he'd be leaving her at an inn and riding out of her life forever. Complicating things between them further would do neither of them any good. But she'd never hated a situation more.

She leaned in to him, soaking in his warmth. The man would be haunting her dreams for many years to come. And she'd relish every memory. She must have dozed off, for when she woke, Jack had pulled the horse to a stop. By the light of the moon she could see the small clearing and the little shack he'd first brought her to. They were back in England. A gnawing pit formed in her stomach. Elizabet had hoped Jack would change his mind about returning her to her home. Hoped he'd ride off with her. They could disappear. She'd rather spend her life with a highwayman she barely knew than the man her parents had chosen for her.

Granted, she didn't know Fergus all that well, either. But her skin crawled whenever he looked at her. The thought of marriage to him... She shuddered. Her life was careening out of control. Then again, she'd never been in control of her own life. If her choices were her own, she'd choose to stay with Jack. As his scullery maid, if necessary. As long as she didn't have to give herself to that snake of a man Fergus. She knew the futility of such a wish. She could hardly stay in this small cottage for the rest of her life, tending the home of a criminal who still hadn't shown her his face.

What did it say if that life sounded better than the one she had waiting at home? She'd been gone nearly a month. Surely, her family presumed her dead. For the first time, she honestly wasn't sure how her parents would react to seeing her again. Relieved perhaps, that their pawn in the marriage mart had been recovered intact? A small part of her missed them. The same part that wished they loved her. But her horror at the choices they persisted in making for her overshadowed that part.

Jack dismounted and reached up for her. She placed her hands on his shoulders so he could slowly lower her down. He kept his arms about her much longer than necessary once her feet reached the ground. She made no move to distance herself from him, quite happy where she was.

He brushed a few errant curls from her cheek that had been loosened by the wind, and she smiled at him.

"Let's go inside," he said, releasing her, a bit reluctantly, she thought.

Things inside the small cottage were unchanged from when she'd seen it last. Smaller than the cottage at Glenlyon. But clean and cozy for all that.

"I'll need to leave in a bit. Only for a few hours."

She spun around and looked at Jack in surprise. "What? Why?"

"I have…a meeting to attend." He came closer, stopping a few inches from her. "I know I canna keep ye here once I'm gone. I could tie ye to the bed…" Her gaze flickered to it and quickly back to him, "but I dinna want to do that. So, I'll ask ye to stay here until I return. For yer own safety, please listen this once. The woods are dangerous, especially at night." He reached out to lightly run his hands down her arms. "I dinna wish to see any harm come to ye."

He could ask her to deliver the moon in a satchel and as long as he asked like that, she'd do her damned best. She nodded. "I will stay put."

He gave her a smile that sent her stomach charging about her belly and put a hitch in her breath. She didn't think he realized that he still held her arms, or that he had pulled her closer. Happy to be there, she certainly had no plans to remind him.

Unfortunately, he realized it on his own and dropped his hands. He cleared his throat and gestured toward the door. "Keep it barred, aye? Ye shouldna have any problems, but 'tis best to be safe."

She nodded, though the first twinge of unease flickered through her. Odd that she felt safer with an outlaw than on her own.

"Ye'll be perfectly safe here," he assured her again. "There is no one near, and the cottage is well hidden in the woods. But just in case, I'll leave ye with this." He handed her a pistol and quickly demonstrated how to use it.

"Bar the door after I leave, and if anyone tries to enter while I'm gone, ye shoot first and ask questions later."

Elizabet nodded, handling the weapon carefully. She still had her knife in her stocking if she needed it.

He took her chin between his fingers and lifted her face back to his. "I have a surprise for ye."

Her eyes widened, and he grinned at her before spinning to hurry out the door. He returned rolling a huge wooden tub and situated it near the fireplace. "I thought ye might like to bathe, since ye'll be alone for the evening. And it was a long journey, after all."

Elizabet clasped her hands together. "Oh, Jack! That would be heavenly. Where did you get this?"

"The village cooper. He crafted a similar tub for making ale. So I had him make one for me."

"To bathe in?"

"Surprised that a heathen Scot might like a bath now and again?"

She shrugged. "Well, if you listen to the gossipmongers at court, yes. Then again, quite a few of them have gone far too long without bathing."

"I pride myself in not being one of the many," he said with a grin. "There's a rain barrel outside this window," he said, showing her. The barrel sat close enough she could scoop bucketfuls of water through the window by leaning out.

"I'll help ye get the tub filled before I go. I need to stoke up the fire and fill the cauldron."

They puttered about the cottage, Jack tending to the fire and emptying the cauldron of water into the tub once it was hot enough, then refilling it and setting it to boil again. By the time the second cauldron of water had heated, the first had cooled a bit. Several buckets of cold water from the rain barrel had the water the perfect temperature. Hot enough to turn her skin a delightful pink without scalding her.

He set a third cauldron on the fire. "So ye can heat yerself back up when the water cools," he said with a wink.

Elizabet's face flamed hot again, and she turned away. Jack chuckled. "Come, my lady. Bar the door behind me. Dinna open for anyone but me. Yer oath on it."

"I promise, Jack. No one but you."

His gaze intensified at that. Even she was surprised the words had left her lips. And somewhat confused as to what she meant by them. He came to her again, drew her close, gazed into her eyes. For probably the hundredth time she wished she could see his face without the mask, look into those eyes without the mystery shadowing them.

"Elizabet," he said, his voice even deeper than usual. He

opened his mouth to say something further but seemed to change his mind. Instead, he leaned down to kiss her on the forehead.

Though not the searing kiss she'd hoped for, even that small touch sent a warmth rushing through her that made her close her eyes and shiver with delight.

He released her, and the loss of him immediately chilled her. She wrapped her arms about herself and followed him to the door.

"I'll return shortly," he said, giving her a long look before departing.

Her stomach tightened with anxiety when he stepped out into the night. She stopped on the threshold, and he took her hand and pressed a kiss to it, lingering much longer than courtesy demanded. Long enough that the lazy circles he drew against her skin with his thumb sent tingles running through her. Long enough she began to want his lips on parts other than her hand.

"I'll be back soon," he said.

"I'll be waiting." The words left her mouth before she'd fully decided to say them.

Her cheeks burned, and the eyes behind his mask widened a bit, but he said nothing. Merely smiled that half smile that made her stomach tighten for entirely different reasons.

He stood waiting until she went back inside. True to her word, she barred the door behind him, smiling when she heard his footsteps moving away after she'd done so. He'd waited until he made sure she'd be locked safe inside.

Elizabet sighed deeply, trying to keep her worry from overwhelming her. She'd never been on her own before, except in her own home in her own room. Even then, the house had been full of servants. Her personal maid, Lucy, slept in a small room adjoining hers. All she'd ever had to do was call out and someone immediately came to her aid. Being on her own, in the middle of a dark forest, with brigands on the loose, would strike fear into even the stoutest heart.

Then again, one of those brigands was her own highwayman. Who'd left her with a pistol and a dagger to defend herself. He'd also left her with a glorious tub large enough she could slump down and actually soak herself in the hot water.

But she'd never be able to enjoy it worrying about Jack. The peril he courted in the dark of night. The carriages he might confront, facing danger, excitement, adventure.

She spun on her heel and marched straight past the steaming tub and over to the window with the rain barrel. A quick peek out the window revealed no one in sight, though she could still hear Jack speaking to someone in the darkness.

"No horses tonight. We can get in and out faster on foot."

"Aye, but we'll have to be quick about it. If we're discovered we'll have the devil of a time getting away."

"We can lose them in the crag above the forest if we're on foot. But if Fergus is with them, we need to risk it. It may be our only chance to discover evidence of his scheme with Dawsey."

"Aye. We best be on our way."

Elizabet didn't wait to hear more. She'd promised, yes. But if Fergus and her father were involved, it affected her more than any of them. And while she trusted Jack with her life, she didn't trust him to share information on their common enemy. It pained her that her father might be numbered among them.

She tucked the gun into the pocket of her dress, gathered her skirts in her hands, and climbed over the sill out into the night. She appreciated that Jack wanted to keep her safe. But she'd had her fill of other people telling her what she could and couldn't do. Once he returned her to her parents, her life as she'd known it would end.

She'd stay out of the way. He'd never know she was there. Perhaps she could help him if he needed it. More importantly, she also needed to see if the stories about him were true. She had her own experience, of course. And tales abounded of the gallant Highland Highwayman who charmed the women so that they willingly gave up their jewelry and who left the men angry and poorer, but intact and unharmed.

But there were those like her father who insisted the reports were only tales. That the Highland Highwayman was nothing more than a typical criminal, as cruel and ruthless as they come. Elizabet didn't believe that of him. But he might act differently when not in her presence.

She would never know unless she saw for herself.

• • •

John waited with his men under the cover of the tree line. The group of men they watched hadn't made much of a move in the last quarter hour. They seemed to be waiting for something. Or someone.

Philip nodded toward the group. "What do ye suppose they're looking for?"

John shook his head. "I dinna ken, but it's something they dinna want to draw attention to."

The men were gathered near the ruins of an old manor house and had been digging industriously for the better part of two hours. Whatever they'd been hoping to find apparently hadn't been there—snatches of angry whispers floated to where John and his men watched.

Will ran up to John. "Rider, sir, from the south."

He nodded. "Good man. Back to yer post, and look sharp." Will nodded and ran back to his assigned spot.

John gave his men the signal to be ready and watched to see who would arrive. Though he already had a sneaking suspicion.

Another quarter hour passed before Fergus Campbell charged up to the group and dismounted. John turned to Philip. "I sometimes hate that I'm always right."

Philip snorted and turned back to watching. Fergus angrily waved his arms about, obviously not pleased at the lack of progress in finding whatever it was he thought was buried on these grounds.

A twig snapped behind them, and John whirled around, sword in hand. Philip flanked him, ready to fight. A small sigh emanated from the bushes and Elizabet's blond head peeked out. John's jaw nearly hit the ground.

"What are ye doing here?" he whisper-shouted.

Philip shook his head and turned back to keep watch. Not before John caught his smile, though.

John waved everyone back to their posts and looked about for Will. Within seconds, the young man came running into the clearing. He looked back and forth between Elizabet and John, his expression of shock so pronounced John would have laughed had the situation not been so serious.

He grabbed the lad by the collar and dragged him close. It was only when they were face-to-face that John noticed the lad's swollen nose and blood-streaked face. "Are ye injured?"

Will stood up as straight as he could within John's grasp. "No, sir."

John's eyes widened and he purposefully glanced at Will's nose. Will sniffled. "A small accident, sir. Nothing more."

Elizabet snorted, but they both ignored her. John decided to let Will's nose go.

"How is it that someone made their way past ye?"

"I'm sorry, sir. I had to…" He glanced at Elizabet, his face turning bright red in the moonlight. "I had to…relieve myself. She must have snuck past me then. I was gone only a minute!"

"That's all it takes, lad. Had she been armed and intent on doing harm, Philip and I wouldna be standing here."

"Aye, sir. It willna happen again."

"See that it doesn't."

He released him to scamper back to his post. Then he turned to Elizabet and crooked a finger at her. She came to him almost as sheepishly, her body moving slowly, though she kept her defiant chin firmly raised.

"What in the devil are ye doing here?" he asked, when she was finally close enough to hear him.

"I overheard you talking about my father and spying on Fergus. What that man does, most certainly affects me. I have every right to be here and see for myself what kind of man I'm marrying. And..." Her gaze faltered a bit before steadying on his own. "I wanted to see what you were doing. Whether the darker stories I'd heard of you were true."

That little statement hurt him far more than he'd anticipated. "Did ye really believe they were?"

"No," she said, head held high. "But I thought it prudent to see for myself rather than rely on the word of others or even my own feelings on the matter. So I followed you here. That's all."

He sighed, unable to fault her logic, as he'd have done the same thing had their positions been reversed. Though that didn't make him like it any better. He took her arm and pulled her in close, stopping short as his fingers slipped across a warm, sticky substance. He pulled his hand away and peered at the dark smear on his fingers, fear spiking through his chest.

"Yer bleeding? Is it yer arm? Are ye hurt?"

"No, no, I'm fine," she insisted, waving him off when he tried to get a closer look. "It's not my blood."

He stopped at that. "Whose is it, then?"

"His," she said, pointing off in the direction Will had

gone.

John's eyebrows rose. "And how did his blood come to be on your body?"

She shrugged. "I startled him when I ran past. He grabbed for me, so I hit him."

"Yer the one who damaged him?"

She made a fist and mimed punching someone. "Right in the nose. He let go fairly quickly after that, though not quickly enough, I suppose." She plucked at the sleeve of her clothing with distaste.

The desire to berate her for hitting one of his men warred with a distinct need to laugh. Though in truth, if she got one over on the lad, he deserved it. John found her actions more impressive than anything else. Dangerous, ill-advised, and aggravating. But impressive. He decided to let the matter drop so he could focus on something far more important.

"I left ye behind for a reason. It's dangerous out here. If yer're discovered…"

"Nothing will happen to me. Besides, this is my land. I have every right to be here."

John dropped her arm, stunned at that revelation. "What do ye mean, *your* land?"

She frowned slightly. "I'm not sure which part you're not understanding. It's my land. Or will be when I marry. The ruins there," she said, pointing through the trees. "I haven't been here since I was little, but I recognize them. It's one of my grandmother's estates. She left it to me as part of my dowry."

He ignored the twinge of unease this news brought. If this property belonged to her, then she likely now realized the location of his hideout, as the cottage had once been the caretaker's lodging on the property until large chunks of the estate had been sold. John's grandfather had bought much of it, because one of their own estates bordered this property.

She made no mention of it, though, and he certainly had no intention of bringing it up. She might not be aware of the cottage, and he didn't feel the need to enlighten her.

But perhaps she could be of some assistance to them. He brought her over to stand near Philip so she could see where Fergus and his group were busily digging again while Fergus shouted insults.

"Do ye ken what they might be looking for?"

She watched them briefly and then shook her head. "There was a fire here some years ago. As far as I know, no one has been back since. The property was never used much even before then. Too far north for my grandparents, though my grandmother loved it. They preferred staying closer to London."

Which meant the property had probably been a prime location for smuggling activities, even more so, if it had been essentially abandoned during the last several years.

"I suppose we've discovered why Fergus is so keen on marrying me."

John's eyebrows rose. "Aye, I suppose so. If this property comes with ye, as ye say, then as yer husband he'd have as much access to it as he'd like. As would yer father."

Her gaze shot back to him. "What do you mean?"

He hesitated to tell her, but at this point keeping her in the dark seemed pointless. "I've been fairly certain that yer father and yon wee bastard have been working together."

Her eyes widened. "Doing what?"

"Smuggling."

She laughed, though there was no humor in the sound. "You must be mad." Despite her words, her forehead creased in a frown, and her gaze returned to the men busy digging up her grandmother's property.

"It would explain why yer father would wed ye to such a man," John said quietly. "These lands border Scotland and have river access to the sea. And being abandoned, little danger of prying eyes. Yer father has probably been using them for years, but with you at marriageable age…"

"He'd lose access if I were to marry, gain control of the property, and decide to do something with it," she said, finishing his thought.

"Aye."

"And if Fergus is working with my father…"

John nodded. "Fergus gains ownership through you, and yer father keeps his access through him."

She shook her head, the sorrowful defeat in her eyes enough to tear his heart to shreds. "So he'd marry me to that monster in order to keep his criminal empire afloat."

John couldn't bring himself to agree, but Philip nodded. "It seems so, my lady."

She looked back at John, her face expressionless but pale in the moonlight. "And you're here to stop them?"

He nodded, and a faint smile touched her lips. "Seems a might judgmental of you."

He nodded again. "Aye. Though it's no' the smuggling that is the problem so much as his methods. There are honorable free traders enough. Men who sell their contraband without murdering and deceit."

"And my father does not."

"Aye."

"Well, anything on this property belongs to me, or will soon enough. And to my family in the meantime. He's stealing and trespassing. I could put an end to this now. Go out there and confront him."

John had to smile at that. He wanted to thrash the woman for disobeying him and putting herself in danger, but he had to admire her spirit.

"That's probably not the wisest course of action."

"And why not? He'd be caught in the act," she said,

jerking her head to where Fergus directed the men loading the boxes they'd finally unearthed onto wagons. "He could be held accountable for his crimes, and we'd both be rid of him."

"Because, lass, while we have several witnesses, we dinna have a lick of evidence."

"The word of the daughter of the Earl of Dawsey should be sufficient," she said, drawing herself up to her full height and putting on that air of entitled nobility that he'd seen often enough in other peers of her station. Though never from her.

"Not when that word is against the Earl of Dawsey himself."

She stepped back as if he'd struck her, not in fear, or even in pain or anger. Her eyes swam with the realization of the truth of his words.

"They would paint ye as a discontented girl telling tales in the hopes of avoiding a marriage to the man her father has chosen. And yer father is, perhaps, more guilty than Campbell. I canna turn over the one without the other."

"But my mother is not guilty. I am not guilty. I am not condoning what my father has done, but he is still my father. And turning him in would put my mother and me on the streets. We'd be ruined."

"My lady…" he said, his resolve for revenge wavering for the first time. He wanted the men responsible for so much death and destruction, for his brother's life, to pay for their crimes. Needed it. The constant, gnawing fire in his gut would never go away until his brother's death was avenged. Until the men responsible were brought to justice.

But what she said was true. If Dawsey fell, so did his family. Still… "What choice do I have?"

"You have a great many choices," she spit out, her body trembling in her anger. "Choices that I, as a mere girl, as you so helpfully pointed out, do not have. There are other ways to ensure my father never harms anyone again. Ways to possibly curtail his activities without forfeiting his standing. Or his life. There are other ways, surely. But you're so blind with your self-styled heroism you refuse to see them."

He opened his mouth to respond but before he could, Will came crashing back into the clearing. "Soldiers, sir! Coming quick, from the south!"

John's men scattered, already well-trained at what to do in just such a situation. Beyond the tree line, Fergus's men did the same, though with much less precision and a great deal more noise and panic. With any luck, the soldiers would focus on those fools while John and his men made it away.

John reached out for Elizabet's arm but she yanked it away. "I'm in no danger from them. In fact, I seem to be the only one within a two-mile radius who *isn't* a criminal."

"My lady, ye're a lone woman, dressed in rags, freely standing in the midst of a band of thieves who are spying on another band of thieves. I dinna believe the soldiers will pause long enough to listen to yer explanations."

She frowned, but he knew she couldn't argue with that.

"Come, we must get ye back to the cottage." He reached out to take her arm again, but she evaded him a second time.

"Elizabet," he said, his patience at an end.

She glanced up at him in surprise, but she still took another step away.

"I know the way back." She sprinted away before he could say another word.

He started to go after her, but Philip grabbed his arm. "We canna lead them back to the cottage! We must follow the plan and meet up at our rendezvous point."

He was right, damn him. Leading them back to the cottage would not only lead them straight to Elizabet, but it would effectively remove the cottage as a safe place to stage their attacks and rest and recuperate when needed. He couldn't return there with soldiers in the area.

But he couldn't leave her to them, either.

"She'll be fine," Philip insisted. "The soldiers are following Campbell's men. They dinna even ken she's here."

No sooner had Philip finished speaking than several soldiers peeled away from the main group and began riding off in the direction of the cottage. And Elizabet.

The king's men should be honorable, above reproach. And if they were to encounter a lady in full finery in the company of her own guard or at least a maid or two, they would most likely be on their best behavior. A bedraggled lass in a torn and bloody chemise alone in a cottage in the woods? No. He'd not leave her to their mercy.

"I have to go, Philip. I'll not let them see me, but I canna leave her to them."

Philip looked fair to bursting with the desire to argue, but he didn't waste any more time. He simply nodded. "Be safe, Cousin."

"Aye, and you."

And with that, John turned and ran. He could only hope being on foot and knowing the territory would be in his favor while the soldiers bumbled through the dark on their horses. He ran faster. Every footfall pounding through the forest thundered in time with his heart.

He had to reach her before the soldiers did.

Chapter Eight

Elizabet shimmied back through the window and dropped the pistol on the chair beside the tub before quickly stripping her clothing. Her bloodstained chemise would be difficult to explain if anyone cared to look closely enough. She looked around for a hiding place that wouldn't be immediately noticed and finally shoved it into the simmering water of the cauldron. It needed to be laundered in any case. Of course, she'd never washed her own clothing before so she wasn't entirely sure how to go about it. But she'd seen the palace laundresses with great vats of boiling clothes, so hopefully it wouldn't appear odd to anyone who might see it.

A loud banging at the door sent a jolt of fear shooting through her, and she clapped her hand over her mouth to keep from screaming. Despite her bravado in front of Jack, his words had hit home. She had nothing to prove her identity. Nothing to keep her safe. For the first time in her life, she had nothing between her and possible danger but her small dagger. At least when Jack and his men had attacked her carriage, she'd had her parents and the drivers. Small help though they were, at least she hadn't been alone.

Still, she was a lady in dire straits. Perhaps if she asked the soldiers for help…

The pounding shook the door, and she grabbed the quilt from the bed and the pistol from the chair near the tub.

"Elizabet! Open the door! It's Jack! Quickly!"

She gasped again, her heart hammering in her chest. Only this time from relief. Whatever their differences, Jack meant safety. That he'd risked his own to ensure hers meant more than she could contemplate. She'd barely lifted the bar when the door flew open and Jack ran in looking like the hounds of hell were on his heels.

"Soldiers are coming," he said, his chest heaving with the force of his breath. "They gave chase…"

"You shouldn't be here!" she said. "They'll find you. Why did you come back?" The terror that rushed through Elizabet nearly paralyzed her with its intensity. Most of it centered on the man before her and the danger that hunted him.

"You have to go," she said.

He cupped her cheek, drawing her close. "I couldna leave ye here alone. If they came…" He swallowed hard and shook his head. "Not all of the king's men are honorable. I couldna leave ye to their mercy."

She covered his hand with her own. "Jack…"

"I promised ye my protection."

"Even at the expense of your own safety?" She shook her head, trying to calm her racing heart. Damn stubborn, wonderful man. She didn't mention the relief coursing through her at his presence. He didn't need the encouragement. "You can't always protect me, Jack."

"That sounds like a challenge, lass."

She sighed and shook her head. "Must you always joke?"

"Always," he said, smiling. He kissed the top of her head, and she shivered against him.

His hands smoothed down over her back, and he seemed to notice her state of undress for the first time. His mouth quirked up into a smile, and he opened his mouth to say something but before he could, hoofbeats echoed through the small clearing where the cottage sat. Men's voices shouted.

"They're here," Jack said.

Bang! Bang! Bang!

"Open in the name of the king!"

Elizabet looked around wildly, fighting the urge to hide under the quilts as she had as a child. Jack was the one with a price on his head. And hiding places were scant, save for under the bed or in the armoire. Two places so obvious they'd be immediately searched.

"Open up or we'll break the door in!"

"Into the water," Elizabet said, running to the armoire to throw open the doors. Then she hurried to the bed, twitching the blankets aside to clearly reveal the floor.

She turned to Jack who stood beside the tub, frowning in confusion.

"Get in the water," she said again. "There's nowhere else. I'll get rid of them."

Something large and heavy crashed against the door, and the wood splintered, but held.

"Do it!" She gave him a shove. "I'm coming!" she said in the direction of the door. "I'll open. A moment, please, I beg you."

She snatched his hat from his head and frantically searched for a place to hide it. Finally, she shoved it behind a pillow on the bed and hoped that she could keep the soldiers from entering the room too far. Jack jumped into the tub, took a deep breath, and ducked beneath the water. He'd be discovered if they got too close, but if they stayed near the door, he couldn't be seen over the lip of the tub and, with the fire in the hearth as the only light in the room, the water would be dark enough to hide him. For a few minutes at least.

She hurried to the door, still clutching the gun in her hand as she tried to keep a grip on the quilt covering her. She threw aside the bar and hurried back, barely in time to miss getting crushed by the door being thrown open. The soldier who had been barreling his way inside stopped short when he saw her. Elizabet knew she didn't look a threat. A lone woman huddling inside a quilt would be no match for a soldier.

He glared at her. "We're looking for an outlaw, a highwayman. He was seen coming this way."

"Well, as you can see, he's not here," she said, hoping Jack could hold his breath for a while longer. She needed to get the soldier out.

"Says you. I need to search to be sure he's not hiding anywhere."

He made a move to enter farther but Elizabet countered his movement, keeping her body blocking as much view of the tub as she could.

"There is nowhere to hide, sir, as you can plainly see. It is a small cottage. Naught to it but this," she said, waving her arm. "The armoire is the only possible place and you can see from where you stand that he is not in there."

The solider looked around, obviously wanting to argue but unable to.

"Under the bed…"

"Bend down. No one is here."

The soldier did as she said, straightening with a frown.

"There," she said, her heart thumping in her chest. She had to get him out, now, before Jack had to surface. Or drown. "You can see no one is here. Get out. Now."

The soldier's attention turned to her, and his look of anger turned to one of a much more dangerous nature as he noticed what Elizabet wore. Or rather, wasn't wearing. He moved a little nearer.

She had no intention of letting him get even an inch closer to her. She brought the pistol out from beneath the quilt. "Get. Out. Now."

The solider scoffed. "Oh, come now. You wouldn't shoot me, would you? I want only to get to know you a little better, that's all. A pretty little thing like you, all alone in the big, dark woods? No man here to protect you."

He stepped closer, his eyes gleaming with evil thoughts. Elizabet didn't wait to see what he intended to do. She dropped the quilt. The soldier stopped in his tracks, his attention riveted to her naked body. Then she raised the gun and shot the floorboards near his feet. The wood splintered, sending a shard up and into the man's calf. He yelped and grabbed his leg, stumbling back out into the yard as Jack heaved out of the water, sucking in a lungful of air.

"Elizabet!"

"I'm okay," she said, her hands shaking. She dropped to her knees to grab the quilt and quickly wrapped it around herself again. More shouts and footsteps.

"Back down," she ordered.

The look of pure astonishment on his face would have been comical if their very lives didn't hang in the balance. But they did, so he needed to obey. Now.

"Quickly!" she commanded.

Jack looked as though she were forcing him to chew molten steel, but he took another deep breath and dropped back below the water. And not a second too soon. A man who looked like he was the one in charge entered with two other soldiers. Elizabet backed up as far as she could without allowing them too far into the room.

The commander glared at her. "What's happened here? Did you shoot a member of His Majesty's army?" he demanded.

Elizabet swallowed her anger. She needed them to leave,

quickly, and arguing wouldn't make that happen. Men such as this liked their women weak and afraid. It wouldn't be too difficult for her to let that show, since her shaky legs were seconds from collapsing beneath her.

"He attacked me," she said. The quilt slipped a bit lower, exposing a shoulder. She clutched it tighter.

The commander's eyes narrowed, and she let him see her trembling lip, her shaking hands. When he took a step closer she let a terrified gasp escape her lips and brandished her pistol.

He held out his hands. "Be careful with that! I'm not going to hurt you, you silly girl. We'll trouble you no further tonight. But this can't go unanswered for. You may have been provoked, but we can't have people going about shooting at officers. What is your name?"

"Mary Smith," she said, giving him the most common name she could think of with her wits rattled as they were by sheer panic.

He seemed about to speak again before the moaning man in the courtyard drew his attention. He sighed. "As you were obviously provoked, I will let the incident go. For now. I would suggest in the future calling for help before firing your weapon."

Elizabet nodded and curtsied, and the commander motioned his men out. The second they were over the threshold, Elizabet rushed forward, slammed the door, and dropped the bar back in place. When she heard hoofbeats riding away from the clearing, she allowed herself to slump against the door with relief.

Jack rose from the water, dripping wet and desperate for air. She stayed put, dragging air into her own tortured lungs. She didn't think she'd breathed the entire time the soldiers were there, terrified they'd discover Jack.

She probably should have run into their arms. Instead of

fighting the urge to run into his. Instead of hiding the man who'd taken her. Who had a vendetta against her family he wouldn't forget. She'd truly chosen sides this time. And looking at the towering, dripping wet, masked man before her, his clothing plastered to him, muscles tensed and ready for a fight—to protect *her*—she didn't regret her decision for a second.

. . .

John stood in the tub and wrung himself out as best he could. His mind raced. He had, for all intents and purposes, kidnapped her. For good reason, yes. But at the end of the day, he was the man responsible for trying to ruin her father, who had gotten her shot and kidnapped. He'd been certain there was something between them, something he grew less capable of fighting. But until that moment, he wouldn't have been surprised had she thrown open the doors and welcomed them in. Instead...

"You didn't betray me," he said.

"No," she murmured.

"Why?" He stepped from the tub, peeled off his coat, and pulled his shirt over his head, dropping them in a soaking heap on the floor. The mask he left in place, though the wet leather chafed against his skin.

Her gaze dropped from his and followed the line of his naked chest. The water ran in rivulets down the hard planes of his stomach. He grabbed the cloth she was going to use to dry herself after her bath and rubbed it across his skin and hair. Her eyes followed each movement. She bit her lip, her breath growing shallow. He took his time drying off. The heat in her eyes as she watched sparked an answering desire in him.

She glanced up and caught him watching. He smiled and

her cheeks flamed bright red and she hastily looked away.

"Why?" he asked again.

She straightened, jutting her pert little chin into the air. "Betraying you wouldn't have helped me much."

"They would have taken ye home."

"You've said you'll take me. I believe you, and I'm not in any particular hurry."

Her words meant more to him than he expected. "Ye believe me?"

She clenched her jaw. "I won't pretend to understand everything that is going on. But whatever claims of your evil deeds may exist, you've not harmed me. You've actually gone to great lengths to see to my comfort. As far as I know, you haven't lied to me. Even when you must have known your words would cause me pain."

He almost flinched from the accusation in her eyes. But he would stand by his plan. Fergus must fall. And so would Dawsey.

"You promised to protect me," she said. "And you have. So yes. I believe you."

Her beauty, standing there in the candlelight, stole the very air from his lungs. In his whole life, he didn't know if anyone had had as much faith in him as she did. He came toward her, and she sucked in a breath when he reached out and brushed her hair from her face.

"Ye're trembling," he said. His fingers lingered on her cheek. He stood so close hardly a breath of space separated them. Heat rolled through him in waves, though he'd spent several minutes submerged in a cold bath. The creamy white of her exposed skin, where the blanket had slipped, flushed pink.

"I'm…" She looked up into his eyes. His thumb brushed across her lower lip, and she shivered. "I'm…cold."

He glanced down and grasped the quilt, pulling it more

tightly against her. "So am I," he said, surprising a laugh from her.

"Come." He took her hand and led her closer to the fire. She sat on the bed while he stoked the flames. "I need to change out of the rest of these wet clothes," he said.

Her mouth dropped open, and she turned around on the bed. He laughed and bent to tug his sodden boots from his feet. He finished peeling off the rest of his wet clothing and reached into the armoire for dry clothes. Though he stood with his back to her, her gaze burned into him. The thought of her watching him while he dressed stirred his blood, inflaming a passion he'd have difficulty containing if he let himself lose control.

Still, he couldn't resist playing a little. If she wanted to watch, he'd give her something worthwhile to see. Though he'd keep his back to her so she couldn't see how much her sitting naked beneath that quilt, watching him dress, affected him.

He pulled on a dry shirt, letting the muscles of his back bunch and stretch as he lifted his arms to let the fabric slide over his body. He made sure the material fell slowly, past his back, over his waist, and finally over his buttocks. A quick intake of breath from the direction of the bed rewarded him for his ministrations. The thought of her sinking her nails into his backside while he moved over her hardened him to the point of pain, and he had the sudden urge to see exactly how she'd react to the knowledge of what she did to him.

He grabbed a pair of breeches, letting his shirt bunch up as he hiked them over his hips, and turned, letting her see him. All of him. She gasped and quickly resumed her perusal of the opposite wall. His chuckle had her cheeks burning so hotly her eyes must certainly be watering.

He sat beside her, the bed sinking beneath his weight. "If you'd like a closer look, I'd be happy to oblige."

Elizabet's breathing sped, causing her chest to rise and fall in rapid succession. He didn't know what had made him offer. Even if she desired him as he did her, and by the heat in her eyes he knew she did, nothing good could come of it. He couldn't keep her. And he wouldn't take her maidenhead and send her back to her family, no longer a virgin and unwed. She would be ruined. He had no qualms about ruining her father. The man was corrupt, cruel, and most likely a traitor. But Elizabet was not her father. And John had no desire to harm her, in any way.

Before he could move away she bit her lip and raised her hand. His forehead creased in a frown, but he didn't move away as she tentatively touched him, brushing her hand along his jaw. She ran her finger along his lower lip as he'd done to her. He sucked in a sharp breath, and the sound seemed to ignite something within her. She leaned toward him.

This needed to stop. Allowing it to continue would be sheer madness. He was a highwayman, an outlaw with a price on his head. A man, not her husband, whose face she'd never even seen.

And she didn't seem to care.

Just one kiss.

Her lips hovered over his, close enough the heat from her skin ignited the desire simmering beneath the surface of his.

Madness, it may be. But he couldn't resist any longer.

He ran his hand through her hair, lightly grasping the nape of her neck to close the distance between them.

His lips touched hers, and she sank in to him. He pulled her close, keeping her captive in his arms while his heart thundered furiously in his chest. Her lips were sweet, soft. She yielded to him, following his lead with an eagerness that made his head swim. This woman embodied every lovely, intoxicating dream he'd ever had. He never wanted to wake.

She moaned, a soft sound that had him threading his

fingers through her hair and nipping at her lip. She opened for him, and he delved inside. His body burned for her touch. She pressed herself closer, wrapping her arms about his neck. She plunged her fingers into his hair and held tight, which only spurred him on. But when she touched the bottom of the mask, he grabbed her hand and pulled away from her, shaking his head.

"No," he said, his voice gruff.

"Why?" she asked, her voice hardly more than a whisper. "Haven't I proven that I can be trusted? That I'll protect you? And your secret?"

The hurt in her voice cut him deep. But there was no help for it. "This is for yer protection, lass," he said. "Ye canna be made to tell what ye dinna ken."

Elizabet searched his eyes and finally nodded. "All right." She sighed and dropped her hand. "As you wish."

He reached up to cup her cheek. "What I wish is of no consequence. 'Tis how things must be."

She nodded, swallowing as though a lump had formed in her throat. Her eyes looked suspiciously moist, and he regretted the pain he might be causing her. But it would save her greater pain later.

He sighed, bringing her closer so he could kiss her forehead.

"Come," he said. "Lie down, *mo maise*."

"What does that mean?" she asked, lying back as he'd asked.

He gave her a gentle smile. "My beauty."

Her heart fluttered. "You find me beautiful?"

"Aye. So much it hurts me just to look at ye."

"Jack," she said, her voice faint.

"Get some rest, lass. It's been a long night. And we'll have to leave at sunrise."

"What? Where are we going?"

He gently pushed her down on the bed and dragged the coverlets over her. "It's far past the time I took ye back."

"Jack…"

But he shook his head. "I've enjoyed our time together. Far more than I expected. But ye have to return. Ye dinna belong in my world."

She flinched at that and he tried again, gently stroking her face. "The soldiers might return. Ye've shot one of them. Even if ye didna kill him, that isna something they can allow."

"And if they return for me, that means my presence is now a danger to you."

"Aye. I suppose. But more importantly, ye're in danger. I would fight for ye, Elizabet, until my dying breath. But even I canna win against so many."

He caressed her cheek and leaned down to gently kiss her. "Rest. I'll watch over ye tonight."

She looked like she'd protest. He understood completely. He'd rather spend their last moments together finishing what they'd started. But that couldn't happen. Too much had happened already. He ached for her. Both in body and soul. But playing with the fire they'd stoked would only end badly for them both.

John moved off the bed and sat in the chair by the fire, turning the clothes drying there. He noticed her chemise swimming in the cauldron and fished it out, laying it out to dry with his clothing. Elizabet rolled to her side and watched him until her eyes began to close.

He remained awake for hours, watching her, committing every breath she took to memory. He didn't want to sleep, but they were as secure as he could make them, and weariness dragged at him. However, instead of retreating to the pallet on the floor as he'd done each night he'd shared a room with her, he climbed into the bed and lay beside her. His arms wrapped around her from behind and pulled her close to his chest. For one night, he'd let himself hold her.

He pressed a soft kiss to her head, and she settled back against him with a contented sigh. He buried his face in her hair, inhaling the sweet fragrance of her. He would forever long for her touch. And crave the lips still pleasantly swollen from his kisses.

Perhaps someday. If things were different. Only he wouldn't pull away when she touched his mask. He'd let her remove it.

And then he'd finish what they'd started.

Chapter Nine

Elizabet watched Jack ride off with a sinking heart. Her real life beckoned. One that included familial obligations, rules, and etiquette. Most definitely not a dashing highwayman who could set her blood to fire with a mere brush of his lips. Jack would live only in her fantasies now. Perhaps she should take to riding around in carriages full of treasure and see if she could instigate another meeting. Though she'd probably succeed in encountering only an outlaw with no sense of honor and gallantry. Jack was a breed unto himself. Any other highwayman she might meet would mean only danger or death for her.

Jack had left her in the dark of night near the main road within sight of a respectable inn. He'd given her more than enough money to hire a carriage and keep the innkeeper from asking too many questions. He'd promised he'd watch her from the tree line until she'd safely entered the inn, protecting her still. But, of course, he couldn't accompany her all the way to her home. Or risk being seen at all.

Arriving home in the wee hours of the morning had

garnered the expected reaction. The sleepy butler had taken one look at her and sent a squealing maid running for her mother. And then all hell had quietly broken loose.

Elizabet knew her parents wouldn't be happy about what had happened but she'd assumed, hoped, that their anger would be aimed at the man who'd taken her. Not that she wanted Jack in trouble, but he wasn't there and knew how to keep himself out of harm's way. She probably should have known better.

Her mother ushered her straight to her room and closed the door before anyone else could enter.

"Tell me quickly. Are you…harmed?" she asked.

Elizabet frowned. "I was shot but my arm—"

"No, no," her mother said, waving that away. "I mean… are you…*intact*?" She whispered the last word as if it were filth coating the inside of her mouth, her face flushing red in the light of the candles.

The temptation to tell her mother that her maidenhead remained intact despite enthusiastic willingness on her part to depart with it burned strong. But the wild look in her mother's eye held her tongue. Barely.

"Yes, Mother. Aside from my arm I have not been harmed in any way."

Her mother heaved a great sigh of relief, and Elizabet resisted the urge to roll her eyes. Gunshot wounds, those were fine. Bullets could enter her as long as a man didn't.

"And your arm is healed now?" her mother added.

"Yes, Mother. It's fine." At least her mother showed some concern over her health, virginity aside, however minimal.

"Well, we'll have the doctor take a quick look. Just to be sure."

She opened the door and invited in the doctor, then sent the maids scurrying in all directions, bringing hot water, linens, food, and tea. Elizabet's surprise at the fuss her mother raised quickly evaporated when she remembered her main value as their ticket out of the poorhouse. In her mother's mind, at least.

Elizabet wanted to argue but knew it would do no good. Nothing she said would matter anymore. She kept her mouth shut, answering the doctor's questions with as little information as possible. Once the doctor confirmed that Elizabet was all right and her wound had healed rather nicely, her mother shooed everyone out again, her concern focused on other things.

"Did anyone see you getting out of the carriage?" she asked.

Elizabet sighed and pressed back against her pillows, closing her eyes. "No, Mother. I don't think anyone saw me."

Her mother twisted the handkerchief in her hands. "I do wish you had chosen a more appropriate time to arrive. What if someone did see you? Arriving in the dead of night, in a strange carriage, completely unaccompanied."

"Arriving in broad daylight would have made more of a spectacle. After all, in the dead of night I wasn't likely to be seen, as most people are in bed sleeping."

"I do not care for your tone, Elizabet. This is a serious matter!"

Elizabet bit her tongue to keep from making any more sarcastic comments. She'd known what she'd be meeting when she arrived home and, aside from the slight display of concern, her family hadn't disappointed her. Her father had yet to even stop in and see her.

"We must keep Mr. Ramsay from discovering anything about this...distasteful business."

Elizabet gaped at her. "I've been gone for more than a month, Mother. Where does he think I've been?"

"We've put it around that you've been ill."

Elizabet's eyes widened with surprise and hurt. "You

didn't tell the authorities? You had no one looking for me?" The small fissure in her heart that had her mother's name on it cracked open wider. "Didn't you care at all?"

Her mother's eyes widened. "Of course we cared. We were trying to protect your reputation! What do you think would become of you if it came to be known you've spent the last month God-knows-where with a man not your husband? And a villainous highwayman at that! Look at what harm a mere hour in his unchaperoned presence did. Offers for your hand virtually disappeared. A whole month with him? You'd be ruined. We had assumed there would be a ransom demand for you."

"And when no ransom demand came?"

Lady Dawsey's lips pursed. Then the fight seemed to drain out of her. "I don't know. I...your father..." She walked over and slumped onto a chair near the bed, leaning back against the cushions with a tired sigh.

Elizabet hesitated to say anything, not sure if she trusted this calmer version of her mother.

Lady Dawsey sat up and took her hands. "My dear child. I know you think I'm some sort of terrible monster, but I have only your best interests at heart. You're home. Safe. Unharmed and unspoiled, by the grace of God."

Elizabet opened her mouth to argue that point but thought better of it. Her shoulder still ached. But she didn't think her mother would appreciate being corrected. And informing her that she was unspoiled only because the highwayman in question had too much honor would most certainly be received poorly.

Lady Dawsey continued. "Fergus Ramsay is a good man with a good family name and connections and enough money to keep you extremely comfortable for the rest of your days. He is even relatively young and handsome, which is a far sight better than most get. There is not a girl around who wouldn't be thrilled to be his wife. I love you too much to risk all of that. Whether it was your doing or not, what happened to you could ruin any chances of your marriage. Mr. Ramsay might have been willing to take you after your accident in the woods, as he himself was there to witness your condition upon being found. But even he would not want you with such a scandal as this attached to your name. All anyone must know is that you were ill."

Elizabet weighed her words carefully. She knew her mother had her future in mind. All their futures. And she couldn't tell her that Fergus would stop at nothing to marry her. She could make love to every member of the king's privy council in full sight of the entire court and Fergus would take her with open arms. As the means to an end, Elizabet had very little to do with why Fergus desired a union with her.

With her father and Fergus set on this union, there would be no escape. She needed to start coming to terms with it.

Elizabet's heart would never pound in her chest when Fergus was near, except perhaps in fear or disgust. She wouldn't dream of him night after night, or find herself staring off into space as she relived every moment of their time together. But she had little choice in the matter. And he would ensure her comfort, if not her happiness. It was more than many women got. No one got the man they truly wanted.

And perhaps if she were to wed Fergus, she could discover his plans, warn Jack if Fergus were planning anything that would harm him. She'd never be with Jack, but if she had to marry Fergus, maybe she could make some good come of it.

Her mother still waited for a response. "I understand, Mother. I know I'm lucky to have Mr. Ramsay. I won't jeopardize our agreement."

Lady Dawsey breathed an audible sigh of relief. "Good. Now, close your eyes and get some rest."

"Yes, Mother."

"Elizabet."

She glanced back at her mother.

"I am truly glad you are home."

Elizabet smiled, warmth spreading through her at her mother's words, despite the ache in her heart left by her highwayman. "I am too."

• • •

John tossed back another whisky and snatched his wig from his head.

"Take care with that, aye?" Philip said, picking it up and placing it on the head form on the table. "We don't have time to repair it before the ball."

"Good. I hate wearing the thing."

Philip raised an eyebrow, and John sighed. "Sorry, Philip. I'm out of sorts today."

"And every day since ye let the Lady Elizabet go," Philip muttered.

John's gaze shot to Philip's. "She has nothing to do with it. I'm merely preoccupied with figuring out a way to prove what that bastard Campbell and Lord Dawsey are up to. Three more bodies were fished from the Thames last night, did ye hear? People who Will tells me had been seen with Fergus earlier in the day and who own an inn that Dawsey is known to frequent. That canna be a coincidence. We must discover the evidence we need to bring them to justice. For all the innocents they've hurt," he said, his voice growing gruff at the memory of his brother.

"Aye. Agreed. But that's no cause for the snit ye've been in these past weeks."

John ignored him and downed another slug of whisky.

Philip shook his head. "It's no' a weakness to admit ye have feelings for the lass."

John's jaw clenched, but finally he shook his head. "Aye, it is. She's Dawsey's daughter. If it werena bad enough that the man is a liar, thief, and traitor to his king, he's had me watched day and night since we returned to London. I dinna ken why. I must ha' done something to raise his suspicions. Or perhaps it's only my name. If he's working with Fergus, they may be planning to pin the highwayman's deeds on me, not even knowing that I *am* the highwayman, simply to harm a MacGregor. Gain the king's favor by turning in a criminal and take down a MacGregor in one shot. They'd not care if it was the truth or not."

"Though it is."

"Aye, but they dinna ken that. Yet. One thing is certain, he'd like nothing so much as to see me fall. Feelings for his daughter would be...ill-advised."

Philip snorted. "It's my general position that feelings for any woman are ill-advised. Be that as it may, ye have them and ye need to deal with them so ye can keep yer wits about ye."

John still wasn't ready to admit anything, out loud at least. "What has any of this to do with tonight's torture?"

"Because it's the first time ye might see the lady since ye let her go. What if she recognizes ye and causes a scene?"

John's heart jumped. A part of him, a very large part, hoped she *would* recognize him. He wanted her to know his true identity. The more rational part of him knew that would be a horrible idea. He'd worn a mask around her for a reason. One word to her father, even unintentionally, and he was done for. No. She could never know the truth.

"I dinna think she'll recognize me. But I'll keep my distance from her to be safe."

Philip watched him carefully until John scowled.

"It would be a far sight easier to avoid her if we simply didna go tonight," Philip said.

"Aye, but showing my smiling face around court as much as possible helps deflect the rumors. Nobody expects the Highland Highwayman to frequent balls and dance attendance on the king. The more I'm seen, the less suspicion is placed on me."

Philip sighed. "Aye, I understand that. I just dinna like it."

"That makes two of us."

"I'd feel better about it all if I didna think ye were still nursing a bruised heart over the lass."

John released an exasperated sigh. "How can I have a bruised heart? We spent only a few weeks together."

"Time has got nothing to do with it. Everyone could see how the two of you were together. If circumstances had been different…"

"But they were not different," John snapped. He took a deep breath and got himself under control. "I healed her, I brought her home. That is the end of it. I havena had any contact with her since, and I have no reason to believe she wants it any other way. It's over. I took care to stay masked in her presence. Even if she were to see me, there's no reason for her to connect the gentleman courtier with the highwayman who took her captive."

"I pray you are right. Because one word from her is all it will take to sow the seeds of suspicion."

John wasn't all that sure Elizabet would say anything even if she did recognize him. She'd had her chance when the soldiers had descended in the cottage… She had feelings for him. He believed. Staking his life on it was a different matter, however.

"It will be fine, Philip."

"Have a care, Cousin. That's all I'm asking. Ye'll never discover what Campbell is up to from the inside of a dungeon."

"Aye, I ken that well. Dinna fash."

Philip shook his head and grinned. "It's too late for that," he said, clapping him on the shoulder. "But I'll try to keep it in check."

John snorted. "That's the best I'll get, I suppose." He grabbed the wig and stuck it back on his head. "Let's get this over with."

John had every intention of keeping his distance from Elizabet. If he even saw her. Her family had been keeping her well secluded since her return. A fact that, while not surprising, had still concerned him. Of course, they'd want to keep her close after her "ordeal." Though he'd been taken aback at the nature of the rumors surrounding her sudden absence from court.

There hadn't been one whisper of Dawsey's run-in with the Highland Highwayman. *That* had been a surprise. He'd been certain Dawsey would be screaming about being robbed by the outlaw the second his runaway carriage had stopped. Instead, not a word about any of it.

Then again, perhaps it wasn't too surprising. After all, if Dawsey mentioned the robbery, he'd also need to mention what was taken. And he probably didn't want to advertise how much money he had, or that he had the habit of carrying it around in his carriage with him. If that were known, John and his men wouldn't be the only band of thieves lying in wait for the man.

As for Elizabet's disappearance, her family had blamed her absence on a lingering illness. The only whispers about the validity of that claim centered around whether she were truly ill, or off somewhere delivering an illegitimate child before returning to court to proclaim her virginal innocence to everyone. She certainly wouldn't be the first young lady to go off and visit a distant relative for a time, only to return with a flatter belly.

The weight of guilt John carried lightened slightly at the

knowledge that their adventure hadn't irreparably harmed her reputation. Though a part of him mourned that fact. Now there were no impediments to her inevitable marriage.

Then he turned and saw her. Standing with another young woman, radiant in a sky-blue gown with a pale-yellow underskirt, laughing as her friend whispered something in her ear. He should leave. Turn his face. Lose himself in the crowd. Something, anything to keep her from seeing him. He hadn't lied to Philip. He really didn't think she'd recognize him. But if he had any wits left in his brain at all, he wouldn't tempt fate.

Instead, he remained rooted to his spot, his eyes locked on her.

And then she looked up. Her gaze passed over him and darted back. Her brow creased, her head tilted ever so slightly to the side, as if she were working out a puzzle. She gave him a vague smile and went back to talking to her friend.

John gasped slightly at the unexpected pain that shot through his chest. She didn't recognize him. That was good. Wonderful. Except for the sharp pain spiking through his shredded heart. Selfish pain he had no right to.

He moved slowly around the room, speaking with acquaintances, making small talk until his head was ready to jump from his shoulders. And all the while, he kept his gaze firmly trained on Elizabet.

He knew he courted danger. Knew the foolish recklessness of his actions. And he didn't care.

The mere sight of her again was worth any price.

Chapter Ten

Elizabet twitched her fan open, sending a faint breeze across her heated face. How she could be so thrilled and excited and yet so full of despair at the same time bemused her. A ball at the palace of Whitehall in London with the merry court of King Charles II would dazzle the most ardent critic. The fact that it might be the last ball she'd attend made the experience bittersweet.

Fergus apparently preferred to devote his energies on murder and mayhem rather than merriment. Or so she'd deduced when he'd informed her of his interest in restoring Rutherdale Hall and spending most of their time there. Had she not been aware of his smuggling operation and her estate's role in his activities, she'd have been very confused by his interest in burying himself so far from the court. Keeping her tongue about it proved more difficult by the day.

The proximity of the estate to Jack's hideout did console her somewhat. Though pointless and foolhardy, Elizabet couldn't help but hope she might catch another glimpse of her highwayman someday. She missed his charming wit, his shameless flirting. Those intense eyes of his focused only on her. The touch of his hand, his lips. Oh, those lips! The strength of his arms about her, keeping her warm, safe.

The music swelled, and she watched the swish of the women's skirts as they danced. She longed to be back on the dance floor herself, but any more exertion and she might make a complete disgrace of herself. She probably shouldn't have had her maid lace her up quite so tight. But Mother had wanted her looking her best. For him. The man she'd soon be shackled to for the rest of her life. Though she doubted Fergus cared much what she looked like, so the effort seemed wasted.

Then again, as he'd failed to make an appearance she could enjoy herself for one more evening. And at least one man seemed to appreciate the efforts that had gone into her dress. Her eyes met his once again, and their icy-blue depths had her heart jumping in her chest. The man exuded a vitality that seemed to draw women to him like bees to a banquet. But he ignored all of them, his attention only on her.

"Alice," she said, nudging her friend in the ribs.

Lady Alice Chivers, belle of nearly every ball they'd attended since they were old enough to lace up their first gowns, turned to her.

Elizabet held her fan high enough to hide her mouth as she spoke. "Who is that man over there?"

Alice looked with interest in the direction Elizabet indicated. "You mean the large one who fills out those breeches so well? That satin is no match for the strapping body it's encasing, is it?" she asked with a giggle.

"*Shh*," Elizabet warned, her eyes darting about for signs of her mother.

"Oh, have a little fun, Bess. You'll have little enough of it once you're wed, that's for certain."

Elizabet sighed. "That's true enough."

"Poor Bess." Alice wrapped her arm around Elizabet's waist and hugged her, her perfect auburn ringlets tickling Elizabet's face. "You must be optimistic. Mr. Ramsay seems the sort to live dangerously, take risks. Perhaps one day he'll take one too many. And then you'll be a rich widow, free to do whatever you please."

"Alice!" Elizabet said, though she couldn't hold back her laugh.

"Oh, you know you've thought it. And if you are too miserable in the meantime, perhaps a discreet dalliance with a sinfully handsome gentleman will cheer you."

Alice nodded in the direction of the man Elizabet had indicated. "He certainly seems taken with you. I wouldn't mind a bit of a distraction with him myself."

Elizabet gaped at her, and Alice winked. "Devilishly handsome, isn't he? And rumored to be richer than Croesus with several sizable holdings and laird of some godforsaken pile of rock in Scotland with a name I cannot pronounce. Lucky for us, he prefers his English roots and stays mainly with the court. Very good friends with the king, though not one to flaunt it. Too bad your parents couldn't have made you a match with him."

Elizabet sighed. "Like most eligible men in court, he'd have expected a decent dowry and a wife without a hint of scandal to her name. Which, apparently, after my 'outing in the woods with a known criminal' and mysterious absence from court for two months afterward, is not me. According to my father, Mr. Ramsay was the only man of any substance willing to take me without one. He's gained enough wealth from somewhere that he's not too concerned with accumulating more. What he still hasn't managed to get is a son. The only thing he's interested in is a new wife young enough to get an heir on and pretty enough to make the deed enjoyable."

"Your father told you that?" Alice asked, horrified.

Elizabet nodded. "Nearly verbatim."

Alice's eyes flashed with fury. "It's too bad the Highland Highwayman is such a gentleman. Your father certainly deserves a harsher lesson."

She released an exasperated breath and nodded at the blond gentleman who was now staring at them with a slight frown. Perhaps Alice's anger had piqued his curiosity.

"That is Laird MacGregor," Alice said.

Elizabet's head jerked up. MacGregor?

"Ah, and it looks as though he's curious about you as well."

But before Elizabet could respond, MacGregor stood before them. He politely greeted Alice and then turned his full attention upon Elizabet. She gazed up the long, muscular length of him, her eyes finally meeting his. He bowed his head, his gaze hidden from her briefly.

He dressed as most of the men at court. Silk hose and knee breeches covered legs that looked as strong as tree trunks. His waistcoat, shirt, and elaborate coat were of the finest material, embroidered and embellished until they gleamed under the light of the chandeliers. His curled wig lay over his shoulders, but there was no hint of powder or rouge on his face. Against fashion, maybe. But it suited him. Even in his finery, he managed to look rugged. Dangerous.

Familiar.

She blinked, her cheeks reddening, but she couldn't look away. Something in the depths of those bright-blue eyes hinted at a power barely restrained. He turned that piercing gaze of his to Alice and bowed politely, tipping his hat. "Good evening, Lady Alice. I trust ye are well."

Alice curtsied, snapping open her fan with a practiced flick of her wrist. "I am indeed, my lord. Allow me to present a dear friend of mine, Lady Elizabet Harding, daughter of

Lord Dawsey."

He focused his attention back on Elizabet. She gave him a shallow curtsy, not sure her knees would hold her if she tried anything deeper.

"Good evening, my lady," he said, his cultured voice flowing through her like molten gold.

That voice…she knew that voice…

He took her hand, bringing it to his lips to press a lingering kiss to its back. His thumb rubbed across her knuckles. Each stroke sent tiny embers swirling through her veins, igniting a heat inside her she'd known before with only one man.

Alice grinned and turned to speak to another gentleman at her side, her presence apparently no longer necessary now that she'd satisfied custom and acquainted them with each other.

"May I say how beautiful ye look this evening, Lady Elizabet?"

The echo of his deep, Scottish brogue rang through her ears. She'd been replaying every moment of her time with her enthralling highwayman over and over in her mind since it had happened. She hadn't been able to forget him. Damn him. She'd never forget that voice. It haunted her dreams, chased her every waking hour. Turned her into a fanciful, scatterbrained chit who wanted nothing more than to hear her name on those honeyed lips again.

And now she had. She didn't have a shred of doubt. The way he said it, with the same inflection, as if he were savoring every syllable on his tongue.

Jack.

She met his gaze again. Those eyes. They were the same eyes that had stared at her so many times. The same eyes that had watched her from behind a worn leather mask. Deep pools of dangerous secrets that tempted her to all manner of folly. Oh, it had been difficult to see their exact hue under the shadow of the mask. But the shape of them, the way they moved when he spoke, couldn't be hidden.

She froze, her body tightening, envisioning those eyes behind a mask, not framed by a long, curled wig and bejeweled linens. An emotion she couldn't name flashed across his features, so quickly she might have imagined it. One thing was certain, though. She recognized him. *Knew* him. And he knew it.

Other than that fleeting look, however, he showed no indication that they'd ever spoken before, let alone touched. Kissed. Slept in each other's arms. He gazed down at her and spouted off some more nonsense in that accented and oh-so-deep voice of his. He took her hand, giving it another light kiss. Elizabet squeezed her hand tighter before she could stop herself.

"I had thought to take a stroll around the gardens. Would ye care to join me?" he asked, his eyes daring her to accept.

Two could play his game. "We've only just met, my lord. I'm not certain my mother would approve."

"What objection could she make? The proper introduction has been made. I'm merely requesting yer delightful company for a turn around the gardens, that I'm certain are well populated, as it's so warm in here."

She fanned herself a little harder, completely agreeing with him on that point. She wanted to go, very much. But the last thing she wanted was either of her parents spotting her with him. They would bring trouble to him for lesser infractions than speaking with her in the gardens.

"Come," he coaxed. "We can even stay within sight of the terrace, if strolling alone with me frightens ye."

Her lips tightened. "I am not afraid of you, my lord. I simply don't make it a habit to go traipsing off with every gentleman who asks. I'm a bit more discerning than that."

"Och, of that I have nay doubt, my lady. It wouldna do to

associate with any poor rabble who would be too far beneath ye, after all."

"That's not at all what I meant," she said, resisting the urge to kick him in the shin. "I simply find the company of some more tedious than others."

His laughter rang out, catching the attention of her mother whose eyes narrowed dangerously as she saw with whom Elizabet chatted.

That laugh. Oh, Jack…you can't hide from me…

"I assure ye, my lady, I am anything but tedious. I will try my utmost to be as entertaining as possible."

He offered her his elbow. Taking it would be a mistake. Not taking it somehow felt worse. His smug smile decided it for her. The man had an uncanny knack for knowing the thoughts in her mind. She'd have to try harder to stay a few steps ahead of him. She took his arm, jutting her chin into the air at his amused surprise. A shiver ran through her at the glint in his eye that had nothing to do with being cold.

They turned, and Elizabet caught her mother's disapproving gaze again. She fought down the bubble of unease that threatened to erupt. They were doing nothing wrong. Harmless. Perfectly acceptable.

Well, harmless might be a stretch. After all, her current predicament could most likely be blamed on the man before her. Both her savior and captor. Under circumstances that had cast a shadow upon her once perfect pedigree. And stolen her heart right along with her father's gold. But she should be safe enough in the palace gardens with courtiers and servants wandering all about. Surely even he wouldn't be so bold as to try anything nefarious with so many possible witnesses. More's the pity. She missed his nefarious ways.

And his company. Young, handsome, and charming, he made her body sing with a mere look. With fiercely intelligent eyes that appeared blue upon first inspection, but without the mask darkening their depths, subtle shades of green were apparent. The man beside her might be a scoundrel, but he made her heart pound with excitement. How many more chances would she have for private conversation with him? Not many. If any at all. So she'd make the most of this opportunity. And enjoy every second of it.

For the price on his head had nothing to do with why her heart pounded so, no matter what lies she might tell herself. Many men had taken her hand, pressed their lips to her skin. Many were scoundrels, some downright criminal. Yet her heart had never soared in their company. Her blood would never heat at the merest brush of her intended husband's hand against her skin. She would never stare at his lips, longing to feel them pressed against her own. In fact, she imagined she'd do quite a lot to avoid Fergus from touching her at all.

"What are ye looking for so intently, my lady?" he asked, the sensation of his breath on her skin as he leaned down to talk to her sent a fine tremor through her.

Why could she not be betrothed to a man such as this? One who would stir her interests and passions? Minus the slight detail of his outlawry, of course. And the small matter of his guilt, according to her father, in causing her family's financial ruin. And, of course, his stubborn quest to see her father brought to justice for his supposed crimes.

Why must she fall in love with the one man who should be her greatest enemy?

She tried to ignore her traitorous body and glanced down, away from his penetrating eyes, shocked at the course of her thoughts. But the imminent announcement of her engagement meant she could no longer hide from it. Once the knowledge became public, she'd be trapped.

He wanted to know what she sought?

"An escape," she whispered. And though she hadn't meant him to hear, the sudden tightening of his hand upon hers told her he had.

"From what?" he asked, his voice intent, almost fierce.

Elizabet looked around. They were alone, protected by hedges on one side, the path winding through shrubs and fountains clear ahead of them. She let go of his arm and turned to face him.

"From the nightmare of a future to which you've condemned me."

Chapter Eleven

John stared at Elizabet, her words unleashing a torrent of unease and concern. "What do ye mean?" he asked. "What nightmare?"

Her hand clenched around her fan until he thought she'd strike him with it. No more than he deserved, surely, for a variety of reasons.

"According to my father, you and your merry band of bandits are the sole cause of our reduced fortunes. While I don't quite believe you are the only cause, I can't deny that you are at least partially to blame, as I was there when you accosted us. As for the other reasons, the smudge on my reputation…well, I am as much responsible and will not fault you for saving my life."

His eyebrows raised in surprise, but she paid him no mind and continued. "My reputation aside, with such a decline in our fortunes, no other gentleman has stepped forward to offer for my hand. Only Fergus Ramsay."

John shook his head. "My apologies, my lady, but I dinna ken what you may mean. If yer father finds himself out of coin, 'tis a pity to be sure, but I fail to understand how I am responsible. And surely ye underestimate your charms, my lady. I have no doubt there are several men who'd be only too happy to offer for your hand."

She let out a short laugh, though there was no amusement in the sound. "Once, perhaps. Before you stripped us of what little we had left. Now, there aren't many titled men who are willing to take a woman with little dowry, a besmirched reputation, and nothing to offer but a family crippled under mounting debts. Mr. Ramsay is the only suitor to come forward. And with my family's situation growing more dismal by the day, I have little choice but to accept him."

Guilt gnawed at John. He'd had no intention of shackling the lady with an unwanted husband, though he had serious doubts his role in the matter had made any difference. Fergus wanted the property that would become Elizabet's upon her wedding. And her father wanted him to have it. Still, she wasn't wrong. There were some who would shun her because of the slight hint of scandal. But for most, her beauty and prestigious family would be enough to overlook a multitude of sins.

Her marriage to Fergus was set because her father wished it so, and for no other reason. His motives should be uppermost in John's mind. Those motives were what had gotten his brother killed. What had sent many more innocents to their graves. Catching Dawsey and Fergus and bringing them to justice should be the only focus of John's concentration.

But something else now overshadowed his purpose. Because the thought of another man, especially that bastard Fergus, sharing Elizabet's bed, filled him with a jealousy that burned hotter than anything he'd ever felt.

And he had no right to feel it.

Yet, the thought of Fergus being within a mile of her

made John's insides twist and shudder.

"Well then, I suppose congratulations are in order," he forced out.

"It would be more appropriate to offer your condolences under the circumstances. Or better still, to offer reparation."

John snorted. She'd wear at him like a hound with a bone until he gave in. Dedicatedly persistent, he'd give her that. "I'm truly sorry if ye find yer circumstances not to yer liking. But I'm afraid ye have me at a disadvantage, my lady, when ye accuse me of being the one at fault. I dinna ken to what ye are referring."

"Oh come now, sir. No one is around to hear us. There's no need to keep up the pretense."

His stood to his full height, pinning her with his fiercest gaze. She didn't flinch, though her nostrils flared slightly and she sucked in a breath. But she didn't back down. And he'd had grown men cower before him when he displayed his displeasure.

He clasped his hands behind his back and did his best to keep his rising temper in check. He didn't fear her. No matter what she thought she knew, she had no proof of anything. Still, rumors were ugly things that tended to spread. He couldn't afford any whispers. She played a game without knowing the stakes. A dangerous game. One that endangered all for whom he cared. One he couldn't, wouldn't, allow her to win.

It had been a mistake to approach her. But he hadn't been able to resist when he'd seen her there, glowing and beautiful like a dove among the crows. She had been beautiful, wet and bedraggled in the forest. Beautiful under the moonlight with a blade to his heart. Beautiful in the candlelight in his cottage. Breathtaking lying naked in his bed. Alluring as no woman he'd ever met before had been. Seeing her tonight had taken him by surprise. Her laughter had drawn him like a moth to a flame, and he'd crossed the room before he'd even thought it through.

And now, it seemed, he would pay for his ill judgment.

She stepped closer. "You know exactly to what I'm referring."

He leaned down, closing the distance between them. She still didn't back down. Despite his anger, he couldn't help but be impressed.

"If ye'd like to accuse me of something, Lady Elizabet, ye'll have to be more specific."

She took a deep breath, her cheeks flushing. "All right, then. If you insist on keeping up the charade, I'll be specific. *Jack.*"

That name on her lips again hit him like a fist to the stomach. He couldn't hide his reaction, and she smiled.

"Or should I call you the Highland Highwayman?"

He stepped close enough she had to crane her neck to keep eye contact. "My name is John. And that is a verra serious accusation, madam."

"John," she said, drawing it out like she was savoring the word. "Well, Jack is a common nickname for John, is it not? Not hard to see why you chose it. And it's not an accusation. It's a fact. You halted our carriage, you stole my family's fortune."

"A fortune that didna belong to yer family. A fortune yer father stole first."

She ignored that and continued, her voice growing softer. "You took me away. Healed me. Protected me."

A smile spread across his lips, despite his best intentions. "I'm no' saying I did, but if I had, would that be considered a crime?"

"No. But your other activities most certainly are."

Oh yes, approaching her had been a mistake. If their time together had affected her even a fraction of how it did him, she'd have known him anywhere. He should have stayed as far from her as possible. Yet seeing her there, how could he?

"And what makes ye think that I, a lord of the realm, would need to engage in such activities?"

She shook her head and shrugged her delicate shoulders. "I have no idea why you would do such things. I know only that you do."

"And how do ye know?"

She swallowed, her eyes fixed on his. "Your voice. You did well deepening your voice. But it's the same. Your laugh. Your stature and bearing. But mostly…your eyes."

"My eyes?" he murmured.

"Yes." Her voice was hardly more than a whisper. "You wore a mask. But your eyes…you can't hide your eyes."

He had to clench his hands into fists to keep from reaching for her. His initial anger and anxiety were still there but overshadowed by something he definitely shouldn't be feeling for a woman who threatened everything he'd worked toward for the last several years.

And he had no idea what to do about it.

"I'm truly sorry, my lady, for whatever troubles yer family is experiencing. But those troubles didna stem from me."

Elizabet's gazed burned into his. "Perhaps not. But they can certainly be ended by you."

John frowned, for once in his life well and truly stumped. "I'd be happy to offer ye my assistance if I may be of some service to ye. Though I dinna see how I might help in this instance."

"It's very simple, sir. Your actions have forced upon me a union I loathe."

"So ye have said."

"I require a husband. A wealthy one."

"Who, ye have told me repeatedly, ye have found."

"Marriage to Mr. Ramsay is…" A fine shudder ran through her, and John steeled himself against the urge to do the same, and against the now familiar twinge of guilt where she was concerned.

"I'm sorry ye find a good match with a wealthy man, who will no doubt leave ye a very wealthy widow in the near future, so distasteful."

He'd be only too happy to ensure her widowhood seconds after the ceremony, but he didn't mention that to her.

"Spoken like a man who will never have to subject himself to the touch of someone he finds so distasteful. Marriage isn't so simple for a woman."

A sudden image of Fergus laying his hands on the unique beauty before him filled John with a nauseating anger. He tried to shove the feeling away. "I still fail to see how it has anything to do with me."

"Don't be so coy, Jack. Your coffers are deep enough to keep my family from ruin, I'm sure. And you are handsome enough, I suppose."

"Merely handsome *enough*?" he asked, ignoring the comment about his wealth. And her use of his nickname. He knew his wealth, which wasn't nearly as great as she assumed, had nothing to do with the way she reacted to him. But marrying her would be dangerous. For both of them.

Her cheeks flushed, the heated blood of her embarrassment staining her delicate porcelain skin.

"I...didn't—wouldn't—shudder at your touch, I think," she said, unable to meet his gaze for the first time since she'd met him.

He brought up his hand and trailed his finger along her cheek and down the slender column of her neck. He drew her to him, his hand firm on her waist. He leaned down to whisper in her ear while she trembled in his arms.

"Oh, ye'd shudder for me, my little hellcat. But it wouldna be because ye found my touch unpleasant, that I promise ye."

His hand cupped her cheek, and he dragged his thumb

along her bottom lip. Her mouth opened in a tiny gasp, and John released her, stepping back before he forgot everything and reminded her exactly how she enjoyed being in his arms.

She blinked up at him, confused. Wanting.

"Perhaps we should return," he said, straightening the lace at his cuffs to give his hands something to do so he didn't reach for her again.

Elizabet's jaw snapped shut, and that pert little chin of hers jutted back into the air. "Battle-ready," was the word that came to mind when she affected that pose. Whatever she was about to say was something he was sure to hate.

"I propose a deal, sir," she said.

"I'm no' interested in making any deals with ye, my lady."

"How do you know? You haven't heard my terms yet."

He cocked an eyebrow at her. "Because I have nay wish to be involved with ye in any way."

She flinched slightly, and John regretted the necessity of his harshness. His lies. But if wounding her pride would make her rethink the folly about to be unleashed, so be it.

"Oh, I think you might change your mind," she persisted.

"I doubt it."

"It's very simple, sir. You are responsible for the predicament in which I now find myself, so you will get me out of it. I require a wealthy husband, and I would have him be of my choosing."

For the first time in his life, John drew a complete and utter blank. He'd expected some sort of blackmail from her, yes. A demand for money. What he'd stolen from her family. At least enough to provide a dowry, perhaps. But marriage? To him? His mind spun. Even more so because the suggestion appealed to him. Much, much more than it should.

"And you would choose me? Why ever for? If, as ye suggest, I'm responsible for yer current plight, why would ye want to shackle yerself to me for the rest of yer life?"

Elizabet sighed. She retained the stubborn set of her chin but a great deal of the fight went out of her. "I don't need to explain all my reasons to you. Call it retribution, revenge even."

"Desire?" he said, not sure why he couldn't resist taunting her.

She pressed her lips together, pinning him with a look that would have worked excellently coming from his old governess. "One word works as well as another. I am out of time. My engagement to Mr. Ramsay will be announced in the coming week. But you, as a great friend of the king, can surely obtain his blessing on our union."

"Possibly. If I had any wish to do so, which I do not."

"Oh, I think you do."

"And why is that?" he said, his voice low, dangerous. He already knew what she was going to say, but he couldn't quite make himself believe she'd really say it.

"It's simple. You will speak to the king and announce our engagement, tonight if at all possible, or I will go to the king myself and tell him how you spend your nights. And I'll be sure to do so before as many witnesses as I can muster."

John froze. "Ye wouldna dare."

"I'm desperate, my lord. I'd do much worse."

"Ye have no proof."

"I don't need any. Even if I'm wrong, and I'm not, the suggestion alone could be enough to ruin you. And I can be very convincing."

Dozens of responses flew through John's mind, and he rejected them one after the other. She was quite correct. There were already rumors floating around court about the true identity of the Highland Highwayman. The mere fact of John's Scottish parentage was enough to turn a few eyes his way. A sworn testimony from a lady in Elizabet's position would finish him, whether she told the truth or not.

He'd considered many possible outcomes to his nocturnal activities. Arrest. Imprisonment. Disgrace. Death. Somehow matrimony had never made the list.

Until now.

She had him right where she wanted him. And she knew it.

Chapter Twelve

Elizabet forced herself to hold his gaze. Not the easiest thing to do when he looked as though he'd rather throttle her than speak to her. She couldn't fault him for that. After all, she had blackmailed him into marriage. Well, almost. She wouldn't rest easy until their plans were made public. Another glance at her soon-to-be husband and she amended that thought. She'd probably never rest easy again.

But once they were wed, she'd be able to help her family. Maybe she could even get her father to cease his criminal activities. And she wouldn't have to spend her nights being groped by that terrifying monster of a man. The mere thought turned her stomach. Instead, she would probably spend her nights alone. Surely Jack—John—would have no desire to have a true marriage with a woman who blackmailed him.

"Did you not promise you'd protect me?" she asked.

He stared at her, his expression unreadable. Finally he nodded. "Always."

She took a step closer. "I have fought, and pleaded, and run off to live with a highwayman," she said with a wry smile.

"All to no avail. Short of murdering the man, a step I'd prefer not to take, I don't have any options left. I may not have a blade to my throat, but if I have to marry that man, I'll be miserable for the rest of my days. I'll pray for death. I can't allow myself to be shackled to him, to let him use me at his whim whenever he wishes. But I can't leave my family to suffer, either, no matter how much they may deserve it. So what am I to do?"

He looked at her, his eyes searching hers for what felt like a very long time. Finally, he lifted a hand and brushed his fingers across her cheek.

"Well," he said. "It seems as though I must go beg an audience with the king."

Relief flooded her, and she released a slow sigh of relief. "Considering the circumstances, it probably isn't appropriate to thank you. But…you do have my gratitude. I know I've forced this on you. And I have no desire to inflict myself on you any more than necessary. Your life needn't change. You are right about my father. I have no doubt he brought much of this on himself. But I had no part in his schemes. And neither did my mother. I merely wish to save my family without condemning myself to a life of misery. Lock me away in some country estate, if you wish. I will not complain."

John stared at her, no sign of what he might be thinking showing on his face.

His silence unnerved her. She pressed on, unable to stop the babbling commentary.

"I simply mean, if there is someone else…or if you wish to seek…companionship…"

His eyebrow rose, and she cleared her throat. Things seemed to be going downhill quickly, but try as she might, she couldn't make it stop. "I mean only to say I know I am not your choice, so if you choose to spend your time elsewhere, I'll not stand in your way."

"Will ye no'?" he said, his voice thick with amusement.

It irked her. How dare he find this funny? "No. I won't. I have no expectation of truly living as man and wife. I desire only your name. Nothing more."

He shook his head. "Oh nay, my lady." He ran his hands up her arms and pulled her close. "If ye wish us to marry, ye will be my wife in every way. You will honor me." He gently kissed her cheek. "And obey me." He kissed the other cheek. "And keep my home in order." His hand trailed down to rest against her neck, his fingers brushing against the pulse at the base of her throat. "And bear my heirs."

Her heart hammered in her chest, but before she could say a word, he bent to brush his lips across hers. "And ye will warm my bed every night without fail."

She couldn't breathe. Her head spun. He'd barely touched her, and she seemed on the verge of fainting. The thought of what sensations he might draw from her within their marriage bed sent a tremor of anticipation down her spine.

His mouth hovered over hers. "And you will enjoy every moment of it, I promise ye that."

She raised her face to his, though she made no move to close the distance between them. She hungered for his kiss. And feared it at the same time. He already consumed her thoughts, waking and asleep. What would kissing him again do to her?

"I still haven't asked," she reminded him.

He cupped her face in his hands. "I think a proposal of marriage is enough of a request to suffice."

Before she could respond to that, his lips closed over hers, igniting her blood and searing her very soul.

He released her so suddenly she stumbled forward, her eyes still tightly closed. Her lips tingled from his touch. If that was a taste of what marriage to him would be like, she could hardly wait for the wedding. Something she'd never anticipated and would certainly never admit to him. Though by his smug smile, he seemed to know exactly what kind of effect he had on her.

"If ye'll excuse me, my lady, it appears I have a wedding to arrange."

He turned away, but Elizabet reached out and grasped his arm. "Wait. How do I know you'll keep your word?"

For the first time, John looked truly angry. "I may be many things, madam, but a liar isna one of them. I've given ye my word. I'll keep it."

She swallowed and nodded her head, somewhat bemused at her mortification at having accused a thief of having no honor. "My apologies, my lord."

He shook his head with an amused sigh. "My name is John. If we are to be wed, I suppose ye should start using it," he said with a smile that was tight, but kind.

"John, is it? Or do you prefer Jack?"

He smiled. "Either will do."

"All right. Perhaps I shall save Jack for our...private moments."

Her face flushed, and he took her hand and pressed a gentle kiss to it. "I'll see ye soon. Elizabet."

• • •

John paced in His Majesty King Charles II's private chamber while the king watched with an impatient lift of his eyebrow.

"John. Sit," Charles said, pointing at the chair on the opposite side of the desk where he sat.

John stopped short, realizing what a horrible breach of etiquette he'd committed, and quickly took a seat. "My apologies, Your Majesty."

"If I didn't know better, I'd say you were nervous."

John gave an unconvincing snort. "Aye, perhaps I am a

little at that."

Charles's eyes widened. "Well, that is something I never thought I'd live to see." Charles's keen eyes watched John. "It's either money or a woman. So, out with it. Which one has brought you here?"

John took a deep breath and spit it out. "I wish to marry, sire."

Charles blinked, probably stunned speechless.

"This is a surprise indeed. I never thought I'd see the day a woman made you want to settle down. Tell me, who is she?"

"Lady Elizabet Harding, daughter of Lord Dawsey."

"That name sounds familiar..."

"Aye, sire. This is why I've come to you. She is soon to be betrothed to Fergus Ramsay, son of Angus Campbell."

Charles's amused surprise faded into the mask he wore when performing some unpleasant task. "If the lady is already betrothed..."

"I had hoped, sire, that you'd..."

"No."

John blinked, surprised at the speed of Charles's response. He'd known gaining the king's approval wouldn't be easy, but he hadn't anticipated being denied quite so quickly.

"But sire, the Lady Elizabet is frightened of the blackguard. He's merely using her to gain her property."

"He is hardly the first man to marry for gain, John. Myself included. In fact, it would be more difficult to find a man who has not."

He was losing his argument before it had even begun. He had to do better, make Charles understand. "Sire, the man is a criminal. He and Lord Dawsey have been embroiled in a smuggling scheme—"

"That is a serious accusation, MacGregor. Do you have proof?"

"Nay, sire. Not yet. But I will..." John cursed himself for

revealing his information before he had the proof to bring a formal accusation, but he hadn't anticipated the king dismissing his request so categorically.

The king shook his head again. "You cannot simply accuse a peer of the realm of such a crime with no proof, John. Neither can you go about breaking betrothals and stealing a man's intended simply because you do not like him. You accuse Ramsay and Dawsey of crimes but have no proof."

"Your Majesty, please…she asked for my help and I vowed to protect her. I canna stand by and watch him abuse her."

"Then you vowed what was not yours to give. Her protection is in the hands of her father until she is wed. If the lady is being mistreated, then her father should be the one looking out for her interests."

John grimaced. "Her father is the one selling her to Ramsay to line his own coffers and further their criminal venture."

"Again, until you have proof, I'll not hear another word about it. As for lining his coffers, this is neither a surprise nor a cause for concern. The match between them is one that brings advantage to both families. That the lady is unwilling is regrettable. But not, I fear, reason to dissolve the contract."

John's head pounded, his heart racing in growing despair. "He cares nothing for what happens to her."

"And you do?"

John gritted his teeth, hating to admit his feelings aloud. He had never wanted the responsibility for her. Never wanted her well-being in his hands. Most of all, he hated the helplessness that already dragged at him. She wasn't even his, and already forces beyond his control were conspiring to do her harm. His powerlessness gnawed at him. This is why he never wanted to be involved with a woman. How could he stand a lifetime of such vulnerability? But he'd promised his protection, his support. And if he were being honest, he'd been lost to her from the moment he'd stopped that damn horse.

So, he steeled his back and spoke the wretched words out loud. "Aye, sire. I do. Verra much."

Charles sighed and shook his head and John hunched slightly, as if he'd been punched in the gut, trying to curl around the pain that pierced him. He hadn't realized how badly he'd wanted the king to agree until that moment.

"I'm sorry, John. Truly. But I cannot agree to what you ask."

"Your Majesty, if ye'd reconsider…" he began.

But Charles held up a hand to stop him. "I'm afraid there's nothing I can do at this point, John. The lady has already been promised to another, the contracts have been drawn, I'm assuming, if the announcement is imminent, all parties agree—"

"Except for the lady herself!" John said, earning a frown from the king. If John could take back the outburst, he would. Angering the king was not the way to go about getting favors granted.

"My apologies, Your Majesty. It's only…she doesna love him, sire."

Charles gave a mirthless laugh. "Since when has that mattered?" He shook his head. "You MacGregors are an odd bunch. And far too entangled with the Campbells to suit me. It wasn't so long ago that your cousin was in here refusing to marry Campbell's daughter despite my decree, and now here you are, begging me to steal a woman from Campbell's son for you. Even if I were so inclined personally, I wouldn't do it. I'll not start another clan war between the MacGregors and Campbells so one girl can avoid a marriage she does not wish."

"I understand. But sire, it's not so simple…"

"Yes, John. It is. The lady is betrothed to another." Charles stood, signaling an end to the conversation. "If you have feelings for this girl, I'm sorry for it. If I could grant you this favor, I would. And if you find proof of your accusations against Dawsey, I'll hear them. In private. But I'll not reignite the enmity between your clans, even for the sake of a friend," he said, clapping John on the shoulder. "What's done is done. Let her go."

John wanted to argue more but held his tongue. It would do no good and could very likely make matters worse.

He bowed as the king left and then stood motionless in the room, his mind spinning. What now? He wasn't really concerned that Elizabet would make good on her threat. Those had been the words of a desperate woman. And he'd done what he could.

Legally, at least.

He spun on his heel and left the king's chambers. If the king would not help them, they'd have to help themselves. He didn't know what they'd do yet. But one thing he did know for certain—Fergus would have her over his dead body.

• • •

Elizabet paced back and forth inside John's chamber. Yes, her presence here was foolhardy at best, but she couldn't wait for him to find her. Her future depended on what he would say when he walked through that door.

"What in the seven hells are ye doing here?" he growled.

Well, that didn't bode well.

"Jack, I..."

"Never ye mind. I dinna care," he said, swinging the door closed behind him and marching over to her. She'd been so preoccupied with worry she hadn't even heard him enter. She tried to gauge his mood, maybe discern how the meeting with the king had gone, but he didn't even slow down. As soon as he reached her, he swept her into his arms. Then his lips were on hers. All thoughts of kings and betrothals and arranged marriages evaporated under the onslaught of his kiss. She wrapped her arms around him and held on for all she was worth.

When he finally broke away, he kept her firmly in his arms, resting his forehead against hers while they both dragged in lungfuls of air.

"Now. What are ye doing in here?" he asked again.

She laughed. "Well, if you'd let me answer the first time… I was waiting for you. To hear the news. What did the king say? It must be good news, yes? With a greeting such as that…"

John released her and walked away, jamming his hand through his hair. Elizabet's stomach dropped to her toes.

"Jack?" she said, her voice hardly more than a whisper.

He sat on the bench at the foot of the bed. "He said no."

"What?" she asked, praying she hadn't heard him correctly.

"He said no," John repeated more forcefully, slamming his fists on his knees before getting up to pace. "He doesna wish to cause more trouble between the clans. He said that what's done is done. Yer father has the right to choose for ye whom he will, and he's chosen that bastard Ramsay, and the king will do naught to help."

"Oh," she said, her voice faint as her head whirled. She sank onto the bench that John had vacated. "Oh."

There was more she wanted to say, more she should say, but she couldn't seem to make anything else come out.

John dropped to his knees in front of her, and she glanced at him, startled. He took her hands in his.

"I am sorry, Elizabet. I thought I could make him see reason."

"You tried," she said, squeezing his hands. "Frankly, I didn't think I'd be able to get you to agree in the first place."

She smiled at him, and John brought her hands up to his lips.

"I canna stand by and watch while ye marry him."

She stroked his cheek. "I didn't think you cared," she said with a small smile, though her heart nearly beat from her chest.

"I didna think so, either."

She stared at him, at this man who had saved her life at least twice and had tried to save her again. For a moment, she'd thought she might get to keep him. Instead, she would belong to Fergus. A small piece of her crumbled and died at the thought. But perhaps she could take something from all this. Something to think back on.

She reached up and cupped John's face, her thumb lightly tracing his cheek. Her heart pounded so furiously it hurt, but she couldn't stop now.

"Jack, kiss me."

His eyes widened.

"Please," she whispered.

He didn't wait to be asked again. He leaned forward and brushed his lips against hers, so gently it nearly drove her mad. She whimpered, wanting more, not sure how to ask for it. John brushed the curls from her face and cupped her cheeks, angling her mouth so he could deepen the kiss.

Elizabet kissed him back, grabbing the lapels of his coat to keep him close. The kiss grew heated, urgent. She leaned back, letting the mattress behind her support their weight as she brought him with her. Her head spun. Whether the pleasant falling sensation was from the kiss or lack of air, she didn't know or care. As long as he never stopped.

She trailed her hands down his chest, savoring every hard ridge and plane she encountered. She helped him shrug out of his coat and unbuttoned his vest. But when she tried to pull his shirt from his satin breeches, he stopped her.

"No," he said, kissing her fingers to take the sting from his words. "We canna go further, Elizabet, as much as I wish otherwise."

She looked deep into those beautiful blue eyes of his, more certain than she'd ever been in her life of what she wanted. "Why not?"

He frowned in sudden confusion. "You are to be married. And not to me."

"I know. I'm to be married to a man who doesn't want me. Who wants to use me to further his own ambitions, to get heirs on, and then throw aside when he's done."

John's grip on her tightened, and Elizabet reveled in it. "That will be my life. And I don't want to begin it with nothing to hold on to. No warm memories to keep me sane. No knowledge of the touch of a man I want, a man who cares for me."

She scooted closer to him, pressed against him so there was nothing between them but a few layers of clothing. "Don't condemn me to that life, Jack. Give me something he can't take from me."

He stared into her eyes so deeply she thought her heart would break. "Aye, *mo chridhe*. Come here then, lass."

She wrapped her arms around him willingly, and he bent and reclaimed her lips.

Fire exploded inside. The desperation bogging her down melted into an urgency she couldn't quell, but he seemed determined to take it slow, savoring every second. He kissed her gentle and deep, stoking a slow-burning, smoldering flame that she didn't think would ever be quenched. The knowledge that every touch was their last burned each delicious sensation into her mind forever. The look on his face when he stripped away her last shred of clothing seared onto her heart. Each caress, each embrace, each kiss was like a brand, marking her as his. Always.

She shut out the thought of anyone or anything else. The only thing that mattered was this moment. With him.

He kissed his way down her throat, his hands leaving a trail of tingling fire everywhere he touched. Her eyes kept fluttering closed under his onslaught, but she fought to keep them open. She wanted to see him. Watch his hands move across her body. Memorize every expression that crossed his face as he gazed at her, tasted her, murmured Gaelic endearments that she didn't understand but would never forget.

This was their first time together. Their only time together. She wanted every second stored away in her memory.

As she wanted him to remember her.

She touched every inch of him, kissing her way across his massive expanse of chest, letting her hands travel downward until she found what she sought.

"*A Dhia*," he said, sucking a breath in through his teeth as he shuddered under her touch. "Ye'll unman me, *mo ghràidh*."

She chuckled, emboldened by the power she suddenly had over him. She doubted she'd ever feel such a thing again.

He captured her hand and drew it over her head, entwining his fingers with hers.

"What does *mo ghràidh* mean?" she whispered.

He paused and stared down at her. "My love," he said, letting go of her hand so he could smooth her hair from her face.

"Am I your love?" she asked, her heart racing too quickly to catch a breath.

His gentle smile pierced through her heart, creating a wound that would never heal. "Aye." He kissed her, soft and lingering. "Ye are my love." He kissed her again. "Always,

always, always."

And when he finally entered her, she welcomed the pain that came with the pleasure. She was his. That special part of her that no other man would know belonged to the man *she* had chosen. The euphoria carried her away until she arched beneath him, her cries muffled by his kiss.

Chapter Thirteen

John gathered Elizabet in his arms, luxuriating in the feel of her against him. He knew he shouldn't have made love to her. But he couldn't resist her. Her whispered *please* had nearly broken him. He'd never regret it. He regretted only that he had to let her go.

She snuggled in to him, and he kissed the top of her head. He didn't think he'd be able to sleep again without her by his side. Though it was the last place she should be. He could never keep her safe enough. The last couple months had proven that nicely. Saving her from the horse had put a stain on her reputation. Saving her from the bullet wound had done even more. Trying to save her from Fergus had likely done nothing but stir up trouble with the man and displeased the king. Finding the proof against her father and Fergus that he so desperately needed would avenge his brother and protect countless lives, but devastate hers. And if she were to be seen with him, what was left of her reputation would be well and truly destroyed. Far from protecting her, he seemed to be making her life worse, one blow at a time.

She let him hold her for a few moments longer before sighing and sitting up.

"I should go before anyone notices I'm gone."

She rose and began to dress. John silently watched her, his thoughts in turmoil. How could he let her walk away? How could he let her stay?

"Elizabet..." he said, not sure what he was going to say. Finally, he sighed. "Have ye considered bearing witness with me against them?"

Her eyes widened and her hands fell from where they'd been straightening her gown. "Of course not. Ramsay, I would happily see fall. But my father..." She shook her head. "I'm not going to defend him. And perhaps, if there were some way to punish him for his crimes without forfeiting his life, or condemning my mother to ruin along with him, I might consider it. But there is no such recourse. Condemn him, and we are all ruined. No matter what her faults—and I'll be the first to admit there are many—my mother does not deserve to suffer for my father's sins. Nor do I. And despite everything..." She swallowed hard and when she continued, her voice sounded young, small. "He's still my father. Yet you'd ask me to not only watch him fall but have a hand in it?"

She stepped back, putting more distance between them. "How can you ask that of me?"

John stood and came toward her. "How can I not? They deserve their fate, Elizabet. Do ye know how many have died because of them? My brother..."

He stopped until he could continue with his emotions in check. "My brother would be alive today but for them. As would countless others."

Elizabet's eyes softened. "I am sorry for your brother. Truly. But I cannot be part of destroying my own family."

"And I canna let his crimes go unpunished."

"Why can't you let this go?"

"He's responsible for my brother's death!"

"And he's my father! It's my family that you are trying to destroy. That you would even ask me to help you destroy them..."

"And it was my family that has already been destroyed. How can you ask me to forget it?"

They stared at each other, at an impasse. Neither could bend. And where did that leave them?

But before he could figure it out, someone banged on the door.

"Open up, MacGregor!"

Elizabet's face drained of all color, and John jumped, certain she would faint.

"My father," she whispered.

John grabbed his clothes, throwing on his breeches and shirt so he could help Elizabet with her gown.

"MacGregor!"

"Aye, just a minute!" John called back, tightening Elizabet's laces as quickly as he could.

Part of him wanted to throw the door open and announce to all the world what had occurred there. Rushing about the chamber like a lad caught with the scullery maid sat very ill with him. But Elizabet didn't deserve the derision that would follow. So, for her, he'd bite his tongue.

"Yer hair," he said, touching the mass of curls that trailed down her back.

She hastily separated her hair into three parts, leaving the curls at the side of her face to hang free and gathering the hair at the back of her head to twist it into a bun. John found a few of the pins and thrust them at her.

The door nearly splintered from the furious banging.

"Out the back," John said, thankful that his room led to one of the many courtyards at the palace.

They rushed to the door, and she reached for the handle, but he pulled her to him, kissing her hard. She clung to him with a small whimper. He couldn't let her go like this. He wasn't sure he could let her go at all.

But he didn't have a choice.

They pulled apart, hearts pounding, breath ragged. She gave him a small nod and a sad smile.

He flung open the door. And stepped back, heart thudding in surprise. His hand reached for the sword that wasn't strapped to his hip.

From the doorway, Fergus saw the gesture and gave him a cold smile, his gaze flicking between him and Elizabet.

"I understand the urge, MacGregor, but you might want to keep your temper in check. Especially as you are not the one who has been provoked here."

Those dark, cruel eyes of his looked back at Elizabet, taking in her rumpled appearance. He shook his head. "Really, my dear, I don't know what I shall do with you. Perhaps locking you away at some small country estate would help curb this wild temperament of yours."

John took her arm and pulled her slightly behind him, a burning rage filling him. Fergus's expression turned glacial. He pushed past John and Elizabet and marched to the other door, throwing it open to admit Lord Dawsey...and four of his personal guard.

Dawsey stormed in. "What is the meaning of this, MacGregor?" he shouted.

Elizabet stepped out from behind John. "Father, nothing is—"

"Not another word, young lady! You have ruined us! Ruined everything! Of all the—"

He took a step toward her, fist raised, and John immediately stepped between them. "If ye wish to live, ye'll back away from her. Now."

Fergus waved a hand as if he could erase the whole scene and moved toward them with an unnatural calm. "Now, now. There's no need for fighting, gentlemen. After all, no permanent damage has been done."

They all looked at him as if he were mad. The fury coursing through John set a fine tremble through his limbs. He'd never wanted to strike anyone so much in his life.

Dawsey was stunned. "What do you mean, no damage? Look at them!"

Fergus's gaze took them in again. "I am. I see my betrothed and an insignificant nuisance who will soon receive his just rewards." He turned his attention back to Dawsey. "All in good time." His gaze raked over her again. "She'll need a firm hand, obviously. But I'm up to the challenge."

John's fists clenched against his sides. But before he could do anything, Elizabet marched up to Ramsay and slapped him right across the face.

If John hadn't been certain of it before, that moment sealed it for him. Good God, he loved the woman.

Fergus, however, did not share his emotion. He grabbed her wrist, squeezing hard enough she cried out. John made to rush to her but Dawsey's guards held him. He fought, but even he could not keep four men at bay. Still, he didn't stop struggling until they'd forced him to his knees.

"I'll call for the King's Guard!" Elizabet shouted, trying to break from Fergus's hold.

Fergus merely laughed. "And tell them what, exactly? That your betrothed forced his way into MacGregor's bedchamber only to find you here, alone with him, and when I took the appropriate action to extricate you from the situation with the full sanction of your father, I was attacked? I hate to be the bearer of bad tidings, my dear, but I'm fairly sure the law, and therefore the guard, will be on my side."

Elizabet tried to pull out of Fergus's grip, her eyes locked on John. Fergus twisted her arm behind her back and hauled her up against him, forcing her to look at him.

"Such spirit," he said, his other hand coming up to grasp her face. "I think I'll enjoy taming you." He bent down and kissed her, squeezing her face to keep her in place.

John roared with rage, his vision dancing in red and black splotches around the edges with the force of the fury that tore at him.

Lord Dawsey stared at Fergus and his daughter, for the first time looking as though the situation didn't sit well with him.

"Gentlemen, perhaps we should discuss this at a later time. Before we draw too much attention to…" He waved his hand to encompass the room. "This…mess."

Fergus stared at Elizabet, then released her. She stumbled back, and John renewed his struggle against the guards. Lord Dawsey nodded at them, and they released him. He made to lunge for Fergus, but Elizabet jumped between them, placing her hand on his chest.

He glanced down at her, and she gave a slight shake of her head. She was right. Now was not the time or place to teach Fergus a badly needed lesson. But the time would come. John drew in several ragged breaths, trying to calm the urge to run the bastard through with his sword. Fergus smiled his snake-grin at John before strolling toward the door.

"Come, Dawsey. We saw what we came to see. Let's let them say their goodbyes. I can be generous when the mood strikes. They'll not see each other after today. And we have business to attend to."

Dawsey's expression cleared. "Ah yes." He pierced John with his gaze. "A certain highwayman who won't be making a nuisance of himself for much longer."

"What do you mean?" Elizabet said.

Fergus shrugged and pinned his gaze on John. "Everyone

leaves a trail. We can't be faulted for following it. Especially when that trail leads to you. Among other things."

Dawsey squinted at his daughter, anger rolling off him in waves. "You are to go straight to your chamber and remain there until I come for you." He glanced at one of his men. "You. Escort her."

The man nodded and turned to her, though he made no move to touch her.

"Perhaps we should discuss moving the wedding up, my lord," Fergus said. "It's apparent your daughter is eager for the benefits of marriage." He leered at her, and Elizabet took a step back. "I'd have her legally bound before she tries to foist some Scottish bastard on me. She evidently needs a firmer hand."

Elizabet trembled against John, though outwardly she showed no sign of fear. She merely raised her impertinent chin high in the air and returned Fergus's stare for stare. As much as he wanted to run Fergus through with his sword, John's pride in his lady beat strong in his chest.

Lord Dawsey glanced at his daughter. "So she does." He didn't say another word, but turned on his heel and left. Fergus nodded at his men before he left, directing one to guard the back courtyard, one the bedchamber door. The one who'd been ordered to take Elizabet waited just inside to escort her to her suite.

Fergus jerked his head at the solider. "Take her," he said. "Quietly." Then he marched off, the fourth man with him to guard his back.

A stampede of emotions almost too strong to contain crashed through John. Helplessness beat at him. He couldn't protect her. Couldn't save her this time.

She buried her head against his chest and took several deep, tremulous breaths, as if she were drawing strength from him. The quaking in her limbs eased but did not subside. He held her tight, his eyes boring into the waiting soldier, daring him to approach. John's choices were simple. Stand aside and do nothing while her father married her off to that sadistic bastard… Or add abduction to his growing list of crimes and carry her off, far away from Fergus and any others who would seek to harm her.

He didn't even need to weigh the options.

He pushed Elizabet from him, lunging at the soldier before the man had a chance to react. His fist connected with the man's temple, and he crashed, unconscious, to the floor. The guard at the door shouted and rushed in. John spun, grabbing a candlestick from the nearby table, and swung it with all his might. He caught the man on the side of the face, dropping him to his knees. One more swing to the back of the head knocked him out.

"Jack!" Elizabet called out.

The soldier from the courtyard had burst in and was bearing down on him. The man's fist slammed into his face before he could react and the pain exploded in his head. Another jab caught him on the jaw. His ears rang. Flashing spots clouded his vision. The man attacked again, but John managed to lock his arms around him and shoved him toward the wall, throwing him against it with a crash.

The man came back swinging, but John ducked this time. He quickly scanned the room for the candlestick, but it was too far to do him any good.

Elizabet rushed them, the fireplace poker in her hand. She swung, catching the man on the back of the knees. He fell with a growl of fury. Elizabet tossed the poker to John and he caught it, swinging it at his attacker before he could strike again. It connected against the man's helmet and the reverberation vibrated up John's arm. But it did the trick. The man keeled over and lay unmoving on the floor.

John turned to the door, slamming it shut, and barring it.

Elizabet threw herself in his arms, her hands feeling him all over, checking for damage.

"I'm sound, lass, thanks to you." He cupped her face and kissed her. "Are ye hurt?"

She shook her head and clung to him again. He kissed the top of her head and then took her hand.

"Come," he said, marching to the armoire and throwing one of his cloaks about her. "We're leaving."

. . .

Elizabet stared dumbfounded at John as he quickly finished dressing. "What do you mean?"

"I mean," he said, tugging on a boot, "that'll I'll no' leave ye here to be abused. We need to leave before Fergus discovers you and his men are missing."

Hope fluttered in her heart. "Then you've decided to abandon your quest for revenge?"

"Justice," he said, pausing to make the point. "I seek only justice."

"Sometimes the line between justice and revenge blur to the point you cannot tell the difference anymore."

He shook his head. "You dinna understand. Ye're too close to the situation."

She sighed. "I think perhaps that applies to us both."

John kept dressing, ignoring her words. "I'm close. I need only a bit more proof. A bit more time. I have papers, enough perhaps to get the king to investigate further. If I had a witness, one of their men. Or catch them in the act. But I'll no' leave you in his hands while I do. I'll take ye away—"

"No."

John stopped short and stared at her with a stunned and hurt look that fractured her heart. "Ye canna wish to stay with him," he said, his voice gruff.

She took a deep breath, trying to calm her pounding heart. But she couldn't let him make the wrong decision. Especially when it wasn't his to make.

"No, I don't. But I won't let you put yourself in danger for me, either."

John raised an eyebrow. "I dinna think ye need to worry."

"Yes, I do." She came to him and took his face in her hands. "I would love nothing more than to run away with you."

He leaned down to kiss her gently. "Then let's go."

"But," she said, pulling away enough she could look into his eyes, "Fergus won't let this go any more than you will. He will look for us."

"He willna find us," John said, nuzzling her neck. "And once I finish gathering my evidence against him and Dawsey, they will pay. And we'll be free."

Still, even now, his desire for revenge remained unabated. Stoked, even. And while she couldn't blame him, she couldn't aid him, either.

She leaned in to him, her eyes fluttering closed. She allowed herself to let go, revel in his touch. Memorize every sensation. The way the stubble on his face scraped across her cheeks. The softness of his lips as he pressed them to her skin. The strength in the arms that held her so gently. She wanted nothing more than to wrap herself about him and beg him to take her away. But she couldn't.

"No," she said, pulling away again. "He may not find us. But he'll find your family."

John stopped at that and looked down at her, a frown creasing his brow.

"They may not know your other identity, but they know John MacGregor's ties to Glenlyon. It will be the first place they go."

"Do ye think Malcolm will stand by and let his home be

attacked?" he asked. "He's repelled the bastard before. He'll do so again, if the need arises."

"Yes. I'm sure he will. But how many will suffer for it?"

John's jaw visibly clenched, and he spun on his heel and strode to the other side of the room and back again, like a caged tiger who'd been provoked.

"Damn it, Elizabet! I'll not leave ye!" he said, nearly growling with the force of his emotions.

The tears she'd tried to hold back began to fall. Before she could respond, Philip rushed in from the courtyard, his eyes wild with panic.

John pulled her to his side. "Philip? What is it?"

"You are discovered. Lord Dawsey…" His gaze flickered to Elizabet. "My apologies, my lady," he said with a little bow before turning back to John. "But Lord Dawsey and Ramsay have uncovered yer identity and compiled evidence against you. They showed all to the king only moments ago. Before the court. The king had no choice but to dispatch the soldiers."

"What evidence?" John asked, his voice low and hard.

"Witnesses, my lord. Villagers who say they've seen ye at the cottage, riding up wearing a mask and leaving again without it."

John snorted. "Nonsense. There are no such witnesses."

Philip shook his head. "Aye, the likelihood they actually saw anything is slim, I'll admit. But since when has that ever stopped someone from bearing witness? If they are paid well enough, they'll say anything."

Philip's gaze darted to Elizabet and back again. "I believe there is even a witness who will swear to having seen ye at the cottage in the company of Lady Elizabet. The commander of the guard had yer quarters searched and found yer mask."

"So that's why the wee bastard was so smug when he found us." John's face hardened. "Who is this witness?"

"A soldier. He's been wounded. Walks with a limp. When he was injured, he was transferred back to the regiment at court. He saw my lady and recognized her. He..." Philip's face turned bright red but he pressed on. "He swears he entered the cottage and encountered my lady in a state of undress. She fired on him and he fled. The cottage is on your lands, John. They drew their own conclusions."

John nodded, and even Elizabet knew what those conclusions would be. Ironic that they had probably paid a fortune for the man to lie and he needed only to tell the truth to condemn them.

"My lord, please. I sent Will to keep watch, but it would be wise to leave. I dinna think even yer friendship with the king can save ye now." He glanced around, noticing the men littering the floor. "Ye'll be hanged for certain."

Elizabet's heart dropped at those words. "Go," she said, turning to him. "You must go. Quickly."

"Ready the horses," he said to Philip. But instead of following his friend, he turned back to Elizabet. "And what of you? Ye refuse to come with me. And I canna leave ye."

That he would even think of her with his life in peril made her heart flip in her chest. And sent fear for him rushing through her, tying her stomach in knots. "I'll be fine. My life is not at stake."

"No," he said, pulling her close. "Just yer happiness."

She leaned in to him. She'd been so close to being able to keep him. So close to all the possibilities loving him offered. "I...I'll find another way. Somehow. Now go."

He pulled her to him and kissed her, sweet and deep. Then he took a deep breath and let it slowly out. "Nay, lass. I'll not leave ye."

She sobbed but tried to push him away. "John. Go. Now."

But it was already too late.

Chapter Fourteen

"Open in the name of the king!" Fists pounded at the door.

John grabbed Elizabet's hand and ran. He pulled her through the courtyard and into the gardens beyond. The stables weren't too far away. They could make it.

The distant sound of his chamber door splintering echoed through the air, and John's heart plummeted. They should have left the second Philip had warned him. But the thought of leaving her had been more than he could do. The time they'd spent together in the cottage had been the best of his life. She'd saved him. In more ways than one. For the first time in years he'd thought of something other than revenge. She made him think of love and life and laughter. And he didn't want to lose her.

But it didn't look like he would have a choice. Soldiers shouted and boots thundered over the ground. Close. Much too close. There was nowhere to run.

"Elizabet," he murmured.

Before he could say another word she spun, pulled his dagger from its sheath at his hip, and pressed her back to his chest. Then she thrust the dagger into his hand and brought his hand to her throat.

Stunned, John froze. The soldiers burst from the hedges and began shouting.

"Drop the dagger!"

"Release the woman!"

John immediately started to comply, but Elizabet grasped his hand and kept it at her throat, though from the soldiers' point of view it must have looked as though she struggled to keep the blade from her skin.

"You aren't getting out of here without a hostage," she whispered to him.

It took him a moment to push past the abhorrence of having a dagger against her tender throat, and then he wrapped an arm around her waist and hauled her close. "You bloody brilliant, beautiful woman," he murmured into her ear.

He began to back them up, shouting at the soldiers to keep back. Philip had their horses ready at the stables. They had only to make it there. And then…he had no idea. He'd need to make himself scarce. With his recent line of work, he had several plans in place for such a situation. But none had included a maddening woman who insisted upon using her body as a shield. He'd throttle her later for risking her neck for him. Right then, however, she provided their only means of escape.

The soldiers glanced at their commander whose face had turned a delightful shade of purple as he watched his prey slip through his fingers. John and Elizabet had reached the point of the path where it curved, leading into a maze of hedges. If they could make it into the maze, they'd be able to turn tail and run. The stables lay not far beyond.

John looked at the commander. "If ye want to keep this pretty neck of hers unmarred, I would suggest yer men remain where ye are." Then he raised a finger to the tip of his hat in a mock salute and pulled Elizabet into the maze. The second they were out of sight he took her hand and they ran.

Hampered by her skirts and thin slippers, Elizabet couldn't run. Not quickly at any rate. Nor could she breathe with the damn corset she wore. After a few minutes, she pulled her hand from his grasp.

"Leave me. They aren't after me. You must go," she said, her breath wheezing from her constrained lungs. "I can't run any farther in this gown. We must part. Now."

He grabbed her about the waist and kissed her, hard and fast. He would have to leave her. And soon. She couldn't go with him when he fled. They might have managed as a pair of lovers hiding from an arranged marriage. Being hunted as a highwayman with a price on his head was another matter. He wouldn't condemn her to an outlaw's life. But the thought of leaving her standing there, never to see her again, went against everything he was.

"Not yet," he said. He bent and picked her up, throwing her over his shoulder.

The shouting from the soldiers drew nearer, and he spun and ran again. Ran until his chest burned with the force of the air leaving his lungs with each breath. They reached the exit of the maze. John could see the stables. He merely needed to reach them. Philip would have the horses ready.

Elizabet…he put her down and took her hand again, pulling her along with him the final few yards. They'd have to say goodbye. For now. But he'd come back for her. In a few weeks, perhaps, he could come back…

He was so intent on reaching the stables, he didn't see the soldier step from the hedges until it was too late. Until he saw the glint of a pistol in the sun. Heard Elizabet scream.

John turned. Her face had gone ashen, eyes wide with fear and horror. Blood stained the front of her gown, the red bleeding into the satin like ink on parchment. *No!* He couldn't lose her now. Not like this!

She reached for him, and he tried to raise his arms. But they didn't seem to work properly. His legs threatened to collapse, unable to hold his weight any longer. He dropped to his knees. She dropped with him.

Only it wasn't her blood marring her clothing. He frowned. Had he been shot then? That must be why the world seemed dull around the edges, why focusing on anything had become impossible. Why Elizabet was crying.

Shouldn't it hurt?

"Elizabet," he said. Only no sound came from his mouth.

He sank down, slumping forward. Elizabet caught him, resting his head upon her shoulder while she pressed against his chest, urging him to lie down so she could put pressure on the wound.

The soldier who'd shot him came forward, shouting at her to move. She looked up, the fury contorting her face magnificent to behold. She more closely resembled a warrior than a heartbroken lass in a ruined dress. The soldier shouted again and drew his sword.

Before John realized what she meant to do, Elizabet reached beneath his coat and pulled his pistol from his belt. She aimed. Fired. And the soldier fell.

The pistol dropped from her shaking hand, and she turned back to John. Without her strength to support him, he collapsed on the ground. She reached for him, the dead soldier forgotten.

"Jack. Stay with me," she pleaded, again pressing her hands to his chest in a futile attempt to staunch the flow of blood. "Help will come. I'll find help."

John shook his head. Help wasn't going to come. But soldiers were. And she couldn't be found with a dead soldier lying at her feet. He might be able to save her. She wouldn't like it. But he'd make her see reason.

He mustered what strength he had left and forced the words from his throat. "Elizabet, listen to me."

"I'm here, Jack. I'm listening." She stroked his hair back from his face with one hand. The other never left his chest.

"Take my gun," he instructed. She looked at the one she'd dropped and he shook his head. "The other gun. In my belt."

He waited until she had it in her hand. Then he took the hand that rested over his heart and pressed it to the pistol as well. She protested, trying to resume putting pressure on the wound. "No," he said. "Elizabet, my love, stop."

At those words, she froze. But the numbing cold already crept through John. They were out of time. She needed to focus on herself.

He took a deep breath that rattled in his chest. "Wait until the soldiers come. They'll be upon us soon. Wait. And then shoot me."

Whatever she'd expected him to say, it hadn't been that. She shook her head. "You don't know what you're saying."

"Aye," he said as forcefully as he could. "I do."

"No." She gritted her teeth, her mouth pressed in a pinched line. "You need a doctor. You'll be fine. I'm not going to…to do that…not to you. No." She dropped the gun on the ground beside him and reached for him, cradling his head in her lap, her hand cupping his face.

"Elizabet…"

"No. Don't make me do this," she murmured. Hot tears spilled from her eyes to land on his cheeks. "I won't do it. You'll be all right. You're strong."

"Hush, lass." He stroked her cheek, wiping away her tears, though more continued to fall. "I'm no' asking ye to do this for *me*."

"Yes, you are. Why else would you want me to do something like that?"

"The soldiers are coming. If they have a witness who swears ye were with me at my cottage, then ye'll be suspect. Especially as ye shot that soldier. And now ye've killed one of their men. No matter who ye are, ye'll have to answer for that. Unless ye tell them I did it. And prove your loyalty to the Crown by shooting me."

She gasped and pushed away from him. "No. How can you think I'd ever—"

"Ye must," he said, putting the last of his energy into making her understand. "I'm done for, Elizabet."

"No," she said, her voice cracking. "No."

"Come here, love." He held out his good arm, and she came back, pressing herself as close to him as she could get. He kissed the top of her head and she lifted her face. He kissed her, slow and gentle, pouring every bit of love he would never get the chance to show her into it. She broke away from him with a sob.

"I'm done for," he said with gentle insistence. "There's no time for you to run. Philip must have been captured, or he'd have been waiting here for us. Ye need to take the gun and when ye see the soldiers, shoot me. Tell them I killed their man there. And ye took my gun and shot me. They'll have to believe ye if they see it with their own eyes."

"Jack. I can't..." Her breath caught, and she pressed the back of a bloodied hand to her mouth. "Please."

"Aye, my love. Ye can. Ye must." His breaths were coming in short bursts now. He couldn't seem to get enough air. Elizabet had taken on an almost ethereal quality. Her face faded a bit, edged in a glowing light. He smiled at her. "Ye look like an angel."

He reached up to cup her face, and she pressed her cheek against his hand. "You can't leave me. I love you," she said, pain coating every word.

His fading heart jumped in his chest. Then faltered.

She turned her face so she could kiss his palm. "You said you were a man of honor. You promised you'd always protect me. Always."

John smiled. "And so I shall, love. With my dying breath."

A faint breeze blew over them, bringing with it the faint echo of the commander and his men.

"Now," John said. He grabbed the pistol from where she had dropped it beside him and pressed it into her hand. Then he used the last of his strength to haul himself to his feet.

She lunged forward, sealed her mouth to his and kissed him with a passion born of love and desperation. Then she wrenched herself away, tears streaming down her beautiful face as she backed away from him. She raised the gun.

The soldiers poured from the maze. John didn't take his eyes from Elizabet, or she from his. He gave her a slow, sad smile.

She pulled the trigger.

A scream of anguish and rage rent the air, the sound ripped from her throat as John crumpled to the ground. The soldiers shouted, rushed at them. Elizabet fell to her knees, dropping the gun to cover her face.

Then John saw no more.

Chapter Fifteen

Elizabet sat despondent, staring out her window. Alice sat beside her. She'd offered her tea, food, diversion, and when Elizabet had refused them all, she'd finally offered her silent companionship. Elizabet was grateful for her company. Being alone in a house with her parents made life unlivable. Even more with her father's gloating. And Fergus's constant attempts to see her. She'd refused, and surprisingly, her father hadn't insisted. Which only made her suspicious.

"Bess, you've got to eat something," Alice said, pushing a tray of small sandwiches toward her.

She looked at the food and shrank away, her stomach revolting at the sight of it. "I cannot. I'm sorry, Alice. I simply cannot." Her voice trembled, and Alice immediately pulled her into a hug.

Elizabet sobbed in her friend's arms. Images of Jack lying on the ground in a pool of his own blood haunted her every thought. Waking or asleep, she couldn't shut out the sight. Couldn't forget the feel of his body growing colder in her arms.

She hadn't shot him. How could she? She'd have sooner turned the gun on herself. But with her screaming like a wild woman, no one had noticed her shot going wide and disappearing through the shrubbery behind John.

But the wound from the soldier had been grievous. And he'd been so cold, so still.

She sobbed anew, her heart rending. Of the soldier she'd shot, the one who'd killed Jack, she hardly gave a thought. Distantly, she worried about that. Shouldn't it bother her that she took a life? Yet he'd been a threat. He'd shot Jack. And now he was gone. But not soon enough to save her love.

Her father marched into the room, took one look at her, and exploded. "Damn you, Elizabet, enough of this! I'll not stand here and watch you make yourself sick over some criminal. I've allowed you to wallow in your self-pity long enough. You will desist with this behavior at once. Mr. Ramsay will be returning in a few days, and you will be presentable and welcoming, or I will throw you out of this house without a cent to your name."

Elizabet's fury grew with every word her father spewed. She slowly stood, her breath coming in short, sharp bursts. "Go ahead," she said, her voice quiet but steady.

"What did you say?" her father asked, his face growing mottled with anger.

"I said, go ahead. Toss me out. I'll manage. But you won't. You need me too much. Who else will you sell off to the highest bidder to refill your pilfered coffers? You can't steal more from your neighbors. You can't embezzle it from your business partners. The tenants on your estates have precious little to give. And without me to tie you to him, Fergus might stop being your ally and start wanting more for himself. You'll have a rival on your hands. So do your worst. John is dead. You can't hurt me anymore."

Her father sneered at her. He couldn't argue back when

she spoke the truth. But the self-satisfied look didn't leave his face.

"On the contrary, my dear. Your John is alive."

Elizabet staggered back a step and reached for the table to steady herself. Alice gripped her hand, providing silent support.

Her father scoffed at her reaction. "Before you go indulging in any fantasies, he won't be that way for long. He's been exposed as a highwayman. People are calling for him to swing from the gallows at Tyburn."

Elizabet steeled her spine, refusing to allow him the satisfaction of watching her lose control despite the tempest raging inside her. "I'm sure you are the chief among those voices, Father."

"The man is a brigand. His friendship with the king and years of service to the Crown may have bought him some leniency, but he cannot go unpunished. Not with the public outcry against him..."

"Fueled by you!" Elizabet burst out. "The public love him. The only people who don't are the ones whose own deeds have given them reason to fear him."

"Says you. Either way, there's no escape for him now. Though if the king is feeling sentimental I suppose they might let him live. If you call life in a dungeon living."

Elizabet sucked in a breath but her father wasn't finished. "Either way, you'll never see him again. If he lives, he'll either be imprisoned for the rest of his life, or exiled. He's a criminal. He deserves to hang."

"By that logic, so do you." The words erupted from her before she could stop them. Alice squeezed her hand in warning.

"Careful, girl," he said, his voice low and deadly. "My need of you extends only so far. I came to warn you to stop this nonsense at once. Reconcile yourself to your marriage.

There are worse fates."

He turned and stormed from the room. Elizabet slumped into her chair and wrapped her arms about herself, trying to drag enough air into her lungs to make her head stop spinning.

"He's alive," Alice said, patting her hand. "Focus on that. He lives."

Elizabet shook her head, trying to breathe past the lump in her throat. "For now. If my father and the others like him have their way, he won't be much longer. And I doubt anyone will be eager to share any news of him with me. I'll never know what befalls him."

"Oh, my dear Bess," Alice said, pulling her forward to envelope her in a cloud of lavender-scented satin and lace. "You only have to tell me what you wish to do, and I'll make it happen."

Elizabet pulled away and wiped at the tears she couldn't keep from falling. "Oh? You'll help me break him out of prison? Or get Fergus out of my life?"

"In an instant! I'd gladly kill Fergus with my own bare hands, and don't think for a second I couldn't do it."

Elizabet choked out a laugh. "Of that I have no doubt."

"It would probably be easier to break John out of prison."

"From the Tower? Impossible."

"Difficult. But not impossible. With his connections, he most likely isn't being held in the dungeons. They'll need to tend to his wounds. Prison, exile, or execution, they seem to want him alive to experience it. Therefore, he'll need to be someplace relatively comfortable and accessible. A few bribes placed in the right hands and a foolproof escape plan and you'll be away in no time."

Elizabet sighed and covered her face with her hands. "If only we really could."

Alice wrapped her arms around Elizabet. She put her head on her friend's shoulder and for once, let herself completely go to pieces.

• • •

John blinked at the harsh sunlight glaring down on him. After several weeks in the Tower, locked up and healing from his wounds, the sun was too bright, though very welcome.

"John, sit, please."

John glanced at King Charles and nodded, sitting in the indicated chair, though he didn't relax.

"I told you to stay out of this mess," Charles said. "But you couldn't let it alone."

John sighed and rubbed his hand over his newly shaven face. He'd had to clean up before entering the king's chambers. Perhaps the only time he'd been grateful for the strict etiquette involved in being in the king's presence. "Your Majesty, I..."

Charles held up a hand. "It doesn't matter what your excuses are, John. Or even if I agree with them. Your arrest was too public, and Dawsey and Ramsay have too much evidence against you for me to overlook this time."

"Evidence they have fabricated!" John said, too forcefully. At Charles's raised brow he sat back in his chair and added, "Sire."

"That hardly matters now. The rumors are rife, and the evidence—falsified or not—is damning. I'm afraid even I cannot get you out of this one, my friend."

John's heart sank, though he had suspected as much. "I understand, Your Majesty. What is to be done with me, then?"

"Well, that depends on you."

"On me?"

"I know not all the accusations against you are false..." He paused when John opened his mouth, his look enough to keep John from speaking. "But I've also looked the other way because, frankly, most of your so-called victims deserved what came to them, and you provided a justice I could not. And because, despite the damage you did to their coffers, you never actually harmed anyone. I cannot do that, in this case, as you stand accused, with half my guard as witnesses, of kidnapping Lord Dawsey's daughter, on not one but two occasions, I'm told. And in your attempt to flee, you killed one of my guard. Neither of these offenses can be dealt with lightly. I've got shouts on all sides to hoist you by your neck."

John blanched, and Charles's look softened. "I'm not inclined to do so. Neither am I willing to lock you in some dank dungeon for the rest of your days. My only other choice is to proclaim your English lands forfeit and banish you from our borders. I would advise against returning to Scotland for the time being. Though perhaps, someday you could go home to your estate there."

Exile? Though a fair sight better than he had cause to hope for, the prospect still weighed heavily on him.

Elizabet.

He'd never see her again. He'd never see his home, his family. Never bring Dawsey and Ramsay to justice. The thought of them roaming free, his brother's death unavenged and countless more at risk, made his stomach roil.

The king raised his hand and beckoned to the guard standing at the door to open it. John surged to his feet when Dawsey and Ramsay entered.

"Sit down, MacGregor," Charles said.

John had completely forgotten etiquette in the face of his enemies' smug faces. "Sire, ye canna let these men roam free."

"You are the one who should be back in irons, MacGregor," Dawsey said. "The only criminal in this room is you!"

"I should have let the soldiers run you through," Ramsay said, trying to appear bored, though hatred blazed from his eyes. "Though I wish I could have seen your darling Elizabet shooting you with your own pistol. I didn't think she had it in her. Perhaps, I should get her something extra special for a wedding gift."

John leaped toward Ramsay, all but growling, and grabbed Ramsay's sword, yanking it from the scabbard to hold it to Ramsay's throat. The soliders shouted at John and rushed for him, but John thought of nothing but the man before him.

"Here is yer villain, Your Majesty! Here is the man who should be in irons at yer feet. He and Dawsey both! I have evidence, sire, more than enough to convince ye of their crimes. I waited only for a witness, so there would be no mistake. But take these men into custody now, and I can show ye the truth of my words, I swear it."

In his mad panic to make Charles understand, to ensure that Fergus did not once again get away, John failed to see Charles's growing anger. His soul-crushing desire to bring Fergus down overshadowed everything.

"You dare draw a blade in my presence!" Charles said.

Too late, John realized his mistake. But Ramsay hadn't. His slow smile seared into John like a slow drip of acid.

John immediately dropped the sword, but the soldiers had already surrounded him.

"Enough of this," Charles said, waving the soldiers away. They tried to protest, but he waved them off again. Had John made such a dumb mistake in the presence of the rest of the court, he'd have been run through on the spot.

"Sire," he said, his body trembling with the desire to wipe the smug grin from Fergus's face. To avenge his brother and keep Elizabet safe forever. "My deepest apologies. But I implore ye, dinna let these men go free."

"This is outrageous!" Dawsey cried, his face growing a mottled purple. "You have no cause to hold us. There is no such evidence as he claims—"

"Aye, there is! Enough to see ye hanged, you and yer foul accomplice."

"Enough!" Charles bellowed.

The soldiers, probably in confusion as to who was the real threat, did the prudent thing and surrounded them all.

Charles sat back in his chair and fixed each of them with a cold gaze before turning his attention to John. "You have told me time and again that these men are criminals of the highest order. Yet you present no evidence to support your claims. They, on the other hand, have provided a great deal of evidence pertaining to your own guilt."

John's blood thundered through his body, in panic or rage, he knew not. All he did know was that his revenge was before him, and he'd not get the opportunity again. He'd likely be hanged or imprisoned. Fergus would never again be in his grasp. If John ran him through now, they'd both die for certain, as Charles would not overlook such a breach twice. Especially when Fergus dropped dead at the king's feet. But if John were to suffer death anyway, he'd gladly take his enemy down with him.

"Do you or do you not have solid evidence, witness or no, that will convict my Lord Dawsey and Mr. Ramsay?"

John hesitated, Elizabet's tearful image in his mind's eye. Elizabet pleading for her father, blackguard that he was, for her sake and her mother's. He wanted Dawsey to pay for his crimes. But he *needed* Ramsay to pay. Needed to avenge his brother with every ounce of his MacGregor blood. He'd minimize Dawsey's involvement, if possible. For Elizabet's sake. But he would not risk losing Ramsay, even if Dawsey must go down as well.

"Aye, Your Majesty. I do."

"Then, if you want justice done, MacGregor, present your evidence or hold your tongue and be sent to the Tower."

It took John a second to realize what the king had said. "Ye'll listen to my petition, sire? Though I have no witnesses?"

"You said you had evidence. Witness or no, present it. If these men are guilty of that which you accuse, they will be dealt with accordingly. Bring forth your evidence."

John's head buzzed. Finally, the moment was upon him.

"Yes, MacGregor," Fergus said, his voice still calm and measured. "Bring it forth. Present the evidence that will condemn me. And Dawsey along with me. And Dawsey's family along with him."

"Silence," Charles said. "Take them to the Tower. They can wait there while MacGregor presents his case. Then we'll see if there is ought to this matter. Escort him to his chambers. You have one hour to gather your evidence," the king said, with a flick of a finger at John.

The soldiers hauled away a shouting Dawsey. Fergus though…Fergus merely stared at John, his face almost serene.

John followed his guard back to his quarters willingly, longing to be alone. He sank into a chair before the fire, his head in his hands. He'd just seen Dawsey and Ramsay dragged from the room to be thrown into the Tower. He should be euphoric. The king would hear his considerable evidence despite no corroborating witness. With one fell swoop, he could gain his freedom, avenge his brother, and see justice done with the punishment of his enemies.

But Fergus's words echoed in his ears. Dawsey's family.

Elizabet.

What had he done?

Her father had just been taken to the Tower. At John's word. To avenge his brother, yes. To save others from the misfortune of meeting Dawsey or Fergus or their henchmen, yes. And yes, even to save his own neck. But at what cost?

He had loved his brother more than anything. He'd spent a long time chasing revenge for his brother's death. But Elizabet…he loved her with his whole being—body and soul. And yet he'd betrayed her at the first opportunity.

He stood and paced the room, his heart in shreds.

What have I done? What have I done? What have I done?

Her anguish-filled face as she'd held him in her arms, declaring her love for him, as he bled out into the dust, tore at him. His brother, God rest him, was gone. Dead and buried and past any pain that anyone might inflict upon him. Elizabet was alive. Needed him. Trusted him. And he'd failed her.

He stopped pacing and strode to the armoire in the corner of the room, kneeling before it to remove a false bottom. He dragged out a small case and brought it to his chair, opening it to rummage through the contents. Everything he'd collected against Dawsey and Ramsay. Documents showing shipments, contacts, bribes. Personal memos to contacts. Even a few letters not so subtly bragging about their activities. Enough to keep the men in the Tower a good long while, if not anything else.

The evidence Charles required of him.

He went through it, separating out the pieces that explicitly implicated Dawsey. The memos, the personal letters. The other papers might point to him if the trail were followed closely. But Fergus had been his hired gun, the one who'd gotten his hands dirty. Dawsey had been smart enough for that. Without the letters, there might not be anything to tie Dawsey directly to Fergus.

John held the stack of papers, his hand faintly trembling. He gripped them until his knuckles turned white and a slight sweat broke out on his brow. And then he opened his hand and let the papers fall. Right into the fire.

Fergus was much more dangerous. More deadly. And more desperate. But he would drag Dawsey down with him,

John had no doubt. So if he turned over the evidence against Fergus, Elizabet would still suffer. John couldn't bring himself to destroy the evidence against Fergus. He needed to be stopped. The man was a murderous bastard, and no community was safe while he roamed free.

But neither could it be John's hand that brought him, and by extension, Dawsey, down. Elizabet would suffer. And John would rather die alone in a filthy cell or at the end of a rope than cause her one moment more of grief.

He placed the box back in the armoire inside one of the drawers rather than back in its hiding place. It would be found. But Fergus would have a slight head start, if he were smart enough.

The soldiers returned to escort John to the king. He left with them, his heart both lighter and heavier at once. He was sorry for what he was about to do. But had he done otherwise, he'd have regretted it for the rest of his days.

Which were sure to be short, judging by the confused and livid expression on the king's face.

"I don't believe I heard you correctly," Charles said. "Do you have evidence to present, or not?"

John took a deep breath. "No, sire. I'm afraid it's been misplaced."

Charles rubbed his temple. "You do understand I'm trying to save your life, *hmm*?"

"Aye, sire."

"I need only a reason to set you free. I cannot do it due to past friendship or royal mercy. You've angered too many at court. Give me my reason. Turn over your evidence. Have the Lady Elizabet sign a document, detailing what she's witnessed at her father's and Ramsay's hands. I but need an excuse to investigate them further and claim unjust sabotage committed against you. You'll have your life. And your freedom."

John's heart thundered so hard blood roared in his ears. This was everything he'd waited for. Worked for. Sacrificed everything for. Revenge and justice were at hand. Finally.

If he convinced Elizabet to bear witness against her own father. Against Ramsay? He knew she would gladly do so. However, the men were linked. They could not destroy one without the other, and Elizabet would never have a hand in her own father's downfall.

Or maybe she would.

He'd nearly died in her arms. He wasn't entirely sure if she knew he yet lived. But she loved him. When he'd lain bleeding in her arms, she'd told him so. Assuming she would be happy to discover he still lived, would she agree to anything he asked? Would she testify against her father? She wouldn't have to satisfy his need for revenge. But would she to save his life? His freedom?

She might.

Could John ask her to?

He sat silent, his heart and mind raging in turmoil. Battling desires branded him. His need to see his brother avenged, to keep others safe from the murderous tyranny that was Lord Dawsey and his hellspawn follower Fergus Campbell Ramsay had burned as a rampaging fire within him since the day his brother had drawn his last breath. He'd devoted his life to their downfall. How could he walk away from that, especially when doing so would buy his own freedom?

But Elizabet…she was an ache in his soul. A hunger that would never be sated. Were he to spend every moment of his life in her presence, he'd still cry out on Judgment Day that they hadn't enough time.

If she felt even a fraction for him what he felt for her, she'd testify against her father. She'd ransom John's life with her own peace of mind. But doing so would destroy a part of her.

And that would destroy a part of him.

He released a breath he didn't realize he'd been holding. "I have nothing to give ye, sire. And I willna ask it of the lady."

Charles raised a royal brow. "We are talking about your life, John."

"I ken that well." He gave the king a small smile. "I suppose I've finally found something that means more to me."

Charles shook his head. "I can't say I've ever found that myself. But, if you'll not reconsider..."

"Nay."

"Then I am sorry, John." The king nodded at the guards who stood near the door, and they came forward to collect him. "I am sorrier than I can say."

Philip stood waiting by the carriage, looking nearly as bedraggled as John.

John climbed up to sit beside him. "The ship leaves tomorrow. I've been given instructions to be on it as soon as possible."

Philip nodded. "It's a mercy you were given that long. That they let you go at all."

John's thoughts strayed to Elizabet as they often did. In fact, he spent every waking and dreaming hour consumed with thoughts of her. But even as a provisionally free man, he could do nothing about it. She needed to stay where she was. Unhappy perhaps, but safe and alive.

Philip's constant glances in his direction began to grate on his nerves.

"What is it, Philip?"

Philip shrugged. "I merely wondered if ye'd be visiting Lady Elizabet before taking ship."

Every ounce of his being cried out *yes!* But John shook his head. "We've already said our goodbyes. Why prolong the pain?"

"Then ye do love her?"

John frowned at him. "What I feel for her makes no difference. I'm exiled."

"But perhaps not permanently."

"That doesna matter. I willna drag her from place to place, ruin her future with the taint of my past. She deserves a better life than that."

They arrived at the docks, and Philip didn't say anything else while they unloaded the carriage, took everything aboard, and got John settled in a cabin.

"Do ye think having Ramsay as her husband is what she deserves then?" Philip said, continuing their conversation as though they'd never stopped talking.

"Of course not. I left the evidence against him. And I'll do my utmost to bring him down before a marriage between them ever takes place. I may be banished from court but I still have some connections. And perhaps now that their smuggling empire is exposed, by rumor if not by law, the union will no longer be so advantageous to either party."

The cabin was tiny, with hardly any room to move. It definitely wasn't built with two large Highlanders in mind.

Philip stared at him until John snapped, "What?"

"I dinna believe Ramsay will let matters as they are stand much longer. Frankly, I'm surprised he hasna dragged her off to church already. Can ye really leave her to that fate?"

"Can I really take her from it? To what? Dinna ye think I havena thought this through? I had little else to do in that prison cell than go over every detail of every plan I could think of. None of them end well for her. What if she were hurt? I dinna ken where I will end up yet. How can I ask her to live a life of such uncertainty and danger?"

"But if ye love her…"

"Aye, all right ye wee prickling bastard. I love her. It is because I love her that I refuse to drag her into the mess my life has become. She deserves better than that. Better than me."

"Perhaps she should be the judge of that."

John gritted his teeth until his jaw cracked. "No. I'll no' have her risking herself for me. It's over, Philip." He sat on the narrow bunk and took a deep breath, the salt air reviving him a bit. "She's feisty, resourceful. She'll manage until we can find out what Fergus is up to and put a stop to him once and for all."

John meant what he said. He couldn't subject Elizabet to such an uncertain life. If she would even want it. He'd asked her to betray her own father. And she'd rightly condemned him for it. Even if she couldn't shoot him.

But…he couldn't leave her completely unprotected. "Watch over her for me, Philip, aye? Send word if she truly needs me."

Philip nodded his head. "Aye, my friend. I will."

John's gut twisted. He should be the one ensuring Elizabet's safety. But he'd done enough harm to her, enough damage to her life. He'd not make things worse. And if there was anyone he trusted near as much as himself or Malcolm, it was Philip. He would watch over her until John could do so again.

He rubbed at his chest, trying like a child might to ease the ache within.

Maybe, someday, it would work.

• • •

A knock sounded on her door, and Elizabet sighed. "I'm not hungry," she said, hoping whoever it was went away.

The door opened, and Elizabet pinned the intruder with a furious gaze. Alice patted her hand again, and a twinge of guilt ran through her at the fearful hesitation in her maid's eyes. She'd never been cross with Lucy before. But she had no wish to be disturbed, and Lucy had been made well aware of that fact.

"Pardon, my lady. But there is a visitor downstairs…"

"I wish to see no one. Send them away."

"My lady, forgive me, but I think you'll want to see this person."

Elizabet was about to send the maid away, but curiosity got the better of her. "Why is that?"

"He didn't come to the front door, my lady. He came to the kitchens and asked for me. He said to tell you," she frowned as though trying to remember the exact words, "his name is Philip and that you have a mutual friend of whom he has news."

Elizabet was already pushing past Lucy, the tiny flame of hope in her heart bursting into an inferno. "Where is he, Lucy?"

"Waiting in the kitchens, my lady."

Elizabet didn't waste time with any more questions. She flew down the back stairs, skirts bundled in her arms, Alice close on her heels. When she saw Philip in the kitchen she stopped short. He was thinner, pale, with dark circles beneath his eyes. He hadn't had an easy time of it. But he was there, free. And smiling.

"My lady," he said, removing his hat as he bowed. Then he bowed to Alice, his eyes lingering.

"You have news?" she prompted. She knew she should probably ask after him. He'd been taken, along with John. But she couldn't wait for social niceties.

Philip's gaze flickered back to her, and he nodded. "He is to be exiled."

Relief and pain flooded through Elizabet with such force her knees gave way, and she sank into the chair Philip had vacated. He would live. But…exile. He would leave England, would never return. She would never see him again. She hadn't thought it possible for her heart to break more than it already had, yet the pain struck her sharp and deep. She clung to the thought of his face, smiling down at her.

"He asked me to give ye this," Philip said, handing her a letter.

"Thank you." She took it and held it close to her bosom. She'd wait until she was in the privacy of her own room before she read it.

"I must leave, my lady. My laird departs with the tide."

Elizabet's gaze shot to his. "So soon?"

"Aye. The king felt it best that he be gone as soon as possible. Hoping it will appease his enemies, I believe."

"Where will he be going?" She wasn't sure she wanted to know. Would it help to know where he would be? Or make it worse?

"Oh, France at first. From there, my laird hasna quite made up his mind. Seems right lost, truth be told. And it could be a long, lonely journey for a man on his own. Though he does have a private cabin on the ship. It's small, to be sure, but I'm sure there is room if he were to find a companion…"

Her heart pounded in her chest, and she looked around the kitchen to see if they could be overheard. Lucy stood nearby, ensuring their privacy. Alice's eyes were so wide her brows were nearly to her hairline.

Elizabet turned back to Philip. "He said he wants me to join him?"

"He didna specifically say so, no. However," he said, before Elizabet could despair too much, "he is an honorable man. He would never suggest ye leave the comfort of yer home for an unknown life with an outlaw. No matter how much he may want ye with him. Especially when he believes ye hate him for what he asked ye to do."

Elizabet sank back in her chair. He wanted her. That's all she needed to know. "Thank you, Philip."

He doffed his hat again and turned to leave. "A few hours, my lady. No more."

She nodded, understanding his unspoken warning. She didn't have much time to make the most important decision of her life.

The second the door closed, Alice whisked her back upstairs, locking the bedroom door behind them.

"Well?" she asked.

Elizabet stared at her, silent, her mind a whirl of emotion.

"Bess! What will you do?"

She shook herself out of it. There was no time to wallow in the storm raging within.

"I haven't much time. I'll need your help if I'm to leave without my father knowing. At this time of day, we are lucky. He won't be home for a few more hours and Mother…"

"Elizabet." Alice took her hands and gently pushed her into a chair. "I know you are overwhelmed with everything, and you probably can't think of anything more than John not being sentenced to hang."

She tried to stand back up. "Well, of course…"

"Please, think things through before you make a decision you can't change."

Elizabet stared at her, openmouthed.

"I will help you in any way I can, no matter what you choose," Alice promised, "but I want to be sure you are making this decision rationally. If you leave with him, there is no turning back."

Sitting in that chair to calmly consider her options went

against everything in her heart. Her hands trembled with the need to run out the door after Philip and not stop until she was back in John's arms.

"What is there to think about, Alice? I love him."

"I know, my dear. And if you choose to run away with him, I will do whatever is in my power to ease your way. But consider what that will mean. Can you leave your home, live as an outlaw? Always looking over your shoulder? Penniless, if the Crown seizes his estates as they most likely will?"

"Why are you asking me this?"

Alice leaned forward. "Because I want you to truly consider the price you might have to pay."

"I would be with the man I love."

"Yes. But you haven't known him long. And he is, in fact, a highwayman. A criminal, no matter what his motivations. Can you trust him? How would you live? What if you were to have children? Can you really give up this life and all you've known for him?"

Elizabet didn't answer right away. Part of her was angry at Alice's questioning. *I love him!* What else mattered?

But despite what she might be feeling, Alice was right. As miserable as her future might be if she stayed at home, it was certain, at least. Fergus would be intolerable, but eventually she might find a way to fight back. Perhaps be of some use to John instead of the hindrance she would probably be if she joined him. Give him some part of the justice he craved. She still wouldn't worsen her mother's lot by betraying her father. But Fergus…she'd give him up in a heartbeat.

With John…she would never know what the next day would hold. Exciting, in some aspects. But the thought of so much left to the fates or chance made her stomach curdle into knots.

And Alice was right. She didn't know him well. If at all. Did she really love him? Or merely the idea of him?

But then other images came to her mind. Other memories. His eyes crinkling with merriment. The man would probably joke if they draped the noose over his neck. Elizabet flinched away from that thought, shoved it to the deep, dark recesses of her mind. She focused on other things. His strength, his loyalty. The sound of his voice…gruff or cultured, depending on the situation, but always *his*. His touch on her skin. His whispered words of love as he held her. His willingness to give up his own life for her, again and again.

Running away with him…she'd lose some things, yes. But she'd have *him*. Forever. And that thought made her heart sing.

"Yes, I can," she finally answered. "If I had to live without him, if I had no choice but to let him go, I'd find a way to go on. I would keep breathing. But little else, I think. I do have a choice, though. And I choose not to lose him. I won't allow him to slip away and leave me. When the soldiers came… he wouldn't leave me. Not even to save his own life. I'm not going to leave him. He *is* my life."

Alice smiled. "Well then. I think we have some packing to do."

Elizabet laughed, her heart lighter than it had been since John had first been taken. She would be with him again. Soon. And this time, no one would separate them.

Chapter Sixteen

Elizabet stood on the dock, mesmerized by the waves that pounded in time with her heart. She took a deep breath and licked the salt from her lips. Whether it came from the sea spraying on her face or from her tears, she didn't know. Leaving Alice had been gut-wrenching. She had been her closest friend and confidante for so many years. The thought of not seeing her again, perhaps ever, was a bitter sadness. But the thought of turning around and going back to her life as though nothing had happened was intolerable. She would miss Alice, desperately. But she couldn't bear to be without John.

"Are you coming aboard, my lady?"

Elizabet looked up at the crewman who'd addressed her and stepped onto the gangplank, pointing to her trunk. "I—"

"No, she is not."

Elizabet looked up. She met John's furious gaze and thrust her chin in the air. She'd known he would object. He was too protective of her by far.

"Oh yes I am." She tried to pass him, but John blocked

her path.

"Elizabet." His harsh whisper nearly broke her heart, but she wouldn't let it deter her. In fact, it made her more determined than ever.

The crewman looked back and forth between the two of them. "Is there a problem, sir?"

"Aye."

"No." They answered at the same time.

Elizabet thrust her satchel into the man's hands. "Please put my bag in my husband's cabin."

She flushed hotly at John's surprised intake of breath but forced herself to keep eye contact with the young crewman until he bobbed his hat at her and scurried back on board. She tried to shoulder past John, but he grabbed her arm.

"I dinna ken what ye think ye are doing, but I'm not going to allow ye to throw away yer life to come traipsing along with me."

"I've never traipsed in my life, thank you very much. And I'm not throwing away my life, Jack. I'm living it, for once."

"Elizabet—"

She rounded on him, her desperation to be with him melting into a frantic anger. "You won't change my mind," she said. She stuck her finger in his face like a nursemaid scolding her charge. "I'm not going to lose you again, do you hear me? If I have to follow you to the ends of the earth, then so be it. But I will never go through that again."

John stared at her and then slowly brought his hand up to cup her face. "My brave, sweet, beautiful lass." He leaned down and kissed her so gently her heart nearly broke all over again. "Ye do me great honor."

Elizabet smiled. "Then let's go aboard, my love. Our future awaits."

She climbed onto the tilting deck of the ship, grateful for the firm grip John kept on her arm. He steered her to where the crewman had disappeared with her bag, drawing her in to whisper in her ear. "Ye told the crewman to place yer belongings in my cabin, which creates something of a problem."

"What problem? I know that I'm not truly your wife yet, but no one needs to know."

He smiled. "Well, aye, that would be wise, however that was not the problem I meant."

"Which would be?"

John stopped in front of a narrow door and opened it. "This is what I meant."

Elizabet crammed her skirts through the door of the tiny cabin and looked around. Light poured in through a porthole. A small desk and chair were against another wall. John's trunk with her trunk atop it sat beside the desk and opposite everything was a very small, very narrow bed. Her eyes lingered on the bunk. John crowded in behind her and shut the door. Suddenly, all Elizabet was aware of was the heat of him against her and the fact that they would be crammed together in this very tiny cabin for several days, at least. Alone.

"Now do ye understand?" he asked.

She shivered at his breath on her neck and leaned back against him. "No. I still don't understand the problem."

"Don't ye?" He turned her around, his hands gripping her arms.

Elizabet licked her lips and prayed she could keep her voice steady when she answered him. "Well, the space is very limited to be sure, but I'm certain we'll manage."

John's chuckle filled the tiny space. "Ye must think me made of iron if ye believe I am strong enough to keep myself from ye when we will be forced to share such close quarters."

It was Elizabet's turn to look surprised. "The thought never crossed my mind."

John pulled her even closer and leaned in to nip at her earlobe. "Nay?"

"We have...indulged before," she said, putting her hands on his chest to keep some distance between them. "I don't expect, or want, you to keep yourself from me."

John's hold on her tightened. "Aye, but I didna wish to presume I ken yer mind on the matter. Succumbing in the heat of passion is quite different from choosing such... recreations, without the benefit of a priest."

Elizabet laughed quietly. "Well, I admit, I have been spending a fair amount of time with a notorious outlaw. I may have picked up a few bad habits."

"Is that so? What sorts of things did this brigand teach ye?"

Elizabet smiled slowly and leaned in to him. "I'm afraid it would be utterly inappropriate to share that with anyone but my husband."

"Ah, so ye still want to marry me?" He leaned down and brushed his lips across hers.

She shivered and rose on her tiptoes to deepen the kiss. His arms wrapped around her waist, lifting her off her feet. The sudden lurch of the ship knocked them off-balance, and they bumped into the door of the cabin. She laughed and then took his beloved face in her hands. "Of course, I still want to marry you," she murmured against his lips.

"Well then. We can quietly take the captain aside, once we are safely out to sea, and ask him to marry us. Or we can wait until we reach France and marry there. Whatever happens between us before we get there makes no difference."

"Because you are my husband."

"And you are my wife."

"The actual ceremony might have to wait a bit, that's all," Elizabet said with a laugh.

John gave her a slow, smoldering smile. "I love ye,

Elizabet Harding."

"That would be Elizabet MacGregor, if you please."

He leaned forward and kissed her. "I pray ye dinna ever regret choosing me."

"I'd never!"

"It may not be an easy life, Elizabet. We won't be able to return. Charles could only help me so far. I maintain some of my smaller holdings in Scotland, but my lands in England are forfeit. We may be able to return to Scotland one day. But even that may be too close for comfort. Will ye be happy never returning home?"

"My home is with the man I love. I will gladly take remote hideaways, flying bullets, and all the uncertainty that has come with loving you, as long as I can lie in your arms every night and wake to you every morning. I will never regret choosing you."

John released the breath he was holding. "I'll try not to disappoint ye," he said, as he claimed her lips once more.

She pulled away long enough to gaze into his eyes. "You never could. As long as I have you. That's all I want."

The ship lurched again and John pulled Elizabet down to the bunk with him. "Well, my love, have me ye shall."

A cry rose from outside the ship, and John went to the porthole to look out. A group of soldiers led by a furious-looking Fergus stood on the dock, shouting at the ship. Answering shouts came which seemed to make Fergus angrier.

"John," Elizabet said, slipping her hand into his. "Am I discovered so soon?"

"Aye, my love. It looks as though ye might be."

She tried to keep her hand steady but couldn't help the slight tremor that ran through her.

John brought her hand up to his lips and gently kissed it. "Nay worries, my love. Look."

He pointed out the window...at the receding shoreline. Hope burst in her breast.

"Does that mean..."

"Aye. We're safe for now. The ship is already underway, going out with the tide. There's no turning her around now, and I doubt Fergus took the time to get the necessary authority to take a smaller boat to meet us."

"We're safe," she said with a smile.

He nodded, though Elizabet recognized the crease in his brow that spoke of his unease. He'd stolen Fergus's prize possession. And Fergus was not a man who would let that go. But for now...she shoved that thought aside and wrapped her arms about her love.

His lips covered hers as the ship left the harbor. Neither of them noticed as England slipped away.

Epilogue

Elizabet stretched her back and put her feet up on a stool, only to yank them away again when crumbling bits of mortar rained down on her skirts. She sighed and brushed them off before hauling herself up to see if she could locate her husband. There was little point in trying to relax, anyway. At least anywhere in a hundred-yard radius of the house. John had the workers in a frenzy, crawling all over the place in an effort to have the main house, at least, fully restored in the next few weeks.

She found him standing in the courtyard, overseeing the re-thatching of a patch of roof that had worn through. He smiled when he saw her. The worn-out tension inside her dissipated, and she went gratefully into his arms.

"And how are ye today, my wife?"

She snuggled in to him. "Growing more unwieldy. I won't be able to move at all soon."

He laughed and placed his hand over her burgeoning belly. "Aye, ye do look as though ye've swallowed an entire bushel of Mrs. Byrd's fresh bannocks."

She gasped and slapped at his arm, but he just laughed harder and pulled her to him for a hearty kiss.

"You really are the most exasperating man," she said, turning to view the work going on.

"Aye, but ye love me anyway."

She grinned. "Aye, that I do."

She sighed deeply and looked around them. The main house was nearly finished. Work had gone quickly since they'd returned home three months earlier, even though only the most trusted of Glenlyon's men had been enlisted to help. John was still a wanted man. The estate was secluded and largely forgotten by most, so it should be safe enough. But the danger always lurked that one day soldiers would discover them and recapture John. Though he had considered it worth the risk to bring his wife home to bear their first child on his family's soil.

She, on the other hand, would rather her husband be safe and sound far from those who hunted him. But he was her husband and the love of her life. She'd go anywhere he bid. Though with a great deal of argument and not until she'd exacted a solemn vow that should they run into danger, John would immediately flee. With or without her and their child.

For the moment, though, she was glad to be back in Scotland. And with the baby due in a few months' time, she did feel much better knowing Sorcha and the Glenlyon women were nearby. Their home was coming along nicely and while the rest of the buildings would take a bit longer, it was the main house they'd been concerned with completing before the baby arrived.

"Do you think they'll finish in time?" she asked, her hands absently caressing her belly.

"They better. Or our bairn will be spending his first night in the stables."

The courtyard was a bustle of activity that sparked a

familiar anxiety. Activity could draw attention.

"Is it safe, do you think?" she asked, moving closer to him. "Should we have stayed away?"

"And let our child be born in exile? Moving from place to place with no home to call his own? No. It was time to come home. We've been gone for more than a year now. I wouldna think anyone is looking for me still. And besides, Charles seized my English estates, but he left Kirkenroch alone. I dinna believe he'll make a great effort to find me again. As long as I keep my feet firmly on Scottish soil."

She looked over their home again. "It's going to be beautiful."

"Aye," he said, his voice filled with pride. "It's a bonny place. Though none so bonny as its lady."

He lifted her hand to his lips, and she smiled up at him, but their peaceful moment was shattered when one of the village boys ran up to them.

"Riders, sir! Two of them."

Fear spiked through Elizabet. John ran to the gates that led out of the courtyard and looked out. She followed behind as fast as she could.

Kirkenroch sat atop a hill but was situated with its back and sides against rock outcroppings and a small forest, with only its front open. It was secluded but well placed to view the surrounding countryside and the one road that led to it.

"Is it soldiers?" Elizabet asked, her chest heaving both from the effort it had taken to move so quickly and from the terror flooding her system.

"No, *mo ghràidh*," he said, reaching back to take her hand. "Dinna fash. One of them is a lass, see?" he said, pointing to the skirts flapping against the flanks of one of the horses. "And the other driving the wagon…it must be Philip. But who…?"

She shaded her eyes and then gripped John's arm. "Is

that…it's Alice!" She waved wildly, excitement bursting through her. It had been nearly two years since she'd last seen her friend and she'd missed her dreadfully.

John frowned. "How did they end up in each other's company?"

The horses trotted to a stop at the gates, and Elizabet was at Alice's side before she'd had a chance to dismount, slinging questions at her so quickly Alice laughed, despite her drawn appearance. She slid down and into Elizabet's arms.

"What is this?" Alice exclaimed, releasing Elizabet long enough to touch her belly.

Elizabet laughed. "John's son, according to him. I say it'll be a girl."

Alice gathered her in another crushing hug. "You look wonderful. And happy," she said, pulling back to cup her face.

"I am," Elizabet agreed, hugging her again.

They stopped exclaiming over each other long enough to glance at the men, who stood staring at them with twin looks of bemusement.

"Not that we are'na glad to see ye both," John said, nodding at them, "but what are ye doing here? Together?"

Alice jutted her chin in the air, and Philip snorted. "Better break out the whisky. 'Tis a long tale."

Acknowledgments

As always, many, many thanks to the queen herself, my amazing editor, Erin Molta, without whom these books would be a conglomerated mess overrun with "justs." Alethea Spiridon, you are the goddess. Always. To my publicists and Entangled team, I am always blown away by how much effort you put into making each book a success. I am so grateful to be able to work with you all! Sarah Ballance, my #creepytwin, oh bestower of spidery terrors, navigating the often crazy days of writing, and edits, and jobs, and families is so much easier when there is someone who GETS IT. My eternal thanks. Though seriously, one more spider and I'm telling Mickey Mouse where you live! Toni Kerr, thank you for your never-ending support! My sweet family, you are my everything. I hope I make you proud. And to my readers, you make it possible for me to do what I love, and I am humbled and grateful for each and every one of you. Thank you!!

About the Author

Romance and nonfiction author Michelle McLean is a jeans and T-shirt kind of girl who is addicted to chocolate and Goldfish crackers and spent most of her formative years with her nose in a book. She has a B.S. in History, a M.A. in English, loves history and romance, and enjoys spending her time combining the two in her novels.

When Michelle's not editing, reading, or chasing her kids around, she can usually be found in a quiet corner working on her next book. She resides in PA with her husband and two children, a massively overgrown puppy, two crazy parakeets, and three very spoiled cats. She also writes contemporary romance as Kira Archer.

Also by Michelle McLean...

How to Lose a Highlander

To Trust a Thief

A Bandit's Stolen Heart

A Bandit's Broken Heart

A Bandit's Betrayed Heart

Romancing the Rumrunner

Wish Upon a Star

Get Scandalous with these historical reads...

LADY GONE WICKED
a *Wicked Secrets* novel by Elizabeth Bright

Nicholas Eastwood is finally about to get everything he ever wanted. As a reward for his service to the Crown, he has been offered the title of marquess. All he has to do is stay scandal-free until the papers are signed. There's just one problem: His ex-lover, presumed dead, is remarkably alive. Now he must find her a husband, so their shared past can stay buried. But scandals never stay secret for long...

THE DEVIL OF DUNAKIN CASTLE
a *Highland Isles* novel by Heather McCollum

Grace Ellington has made a home in Scotland, but to escape the meddling people who believe she needs to wed, she volunteers to journey north to help a friend in need. Keir MacKinnon has been raised to strike fear in people, on and off the battlefield. Caught in a Highland blizzard with the feisty Grace, Keir realizes the beautiful woman who saved him can also save his nephew's life, so he kidnaps her. Sparks fly, and Grace's courage is put to the ultimate test.

THE ROGUE'S CONQUEST
a *Townsends* novel by Lily Maxton

Former prizefighter James MacGregor wants to be a gentleman, like the men he trains in his boxing saloon. A chance encounter with Eleanor Townsend gives him the leverage he needs. She'll gain him entry to high society and help him with his atrocious manners, and in return, he won't reveal her secret. It's the perfect arrangement. At least until the sparks between them become more than just their personalities clashing.

9 781984 381941